5/21/77

Margaret Mary Moscato
From: Aunt Ann
For First Holy Communion

THE BOBBSEY TWINS

AND THE CEDAR CAMP MYSTERY

The Bobbsey twins travel north of the border for their latest adventure, in Ontario, Canada, where they solve the puzzle of the "Four-winged Blackbird."

What did Tommy Cheechoo, a Cree Indian living on Mr. Bobbsey's land, mean by his warning? When the Bobbseys arrive at Cedar Camp, they find Tommy missing. Has the "Four-winged Blackbird" carried him away? With an Indian boy to guide them and a tame wolf to protect them, the Bobbsey twins search for Tommy Cheechoo. They find many strange things in the Canadian woods—a carved stone that looks like an evil spirit, fool's gold, and real gold—buried in sacks which have disappeared when the police come to check.

But before they go home, the Bobbseys not only manage to find Tommy but also discover the meaning of his message: "Beware Four-winged Blackbird!"

THE BOBBSEY TWINS
By Laura Lee Hope

"Lobo, you're wonderful!" Flossie cried

The
Bobbsey Twins
and the
Cedar Camp
Mystery

By

LAURA LEE HOPE

GROSSET & DUNLAP
Publishers   *New York*

ISBN: 0–448–08014–1

PRINTED IN THE UNITED STATES OF AMERICA
LIBRARY OF CONGRESS CATALOG CARD NO. 67–24237
The Bobbsey Twins and the Cedar Camp Mystery

CONTENTS

CHAPTER I

THE VISITING WOLF

"BERT, Nan! We've found a new dog!" cried Flossie Bobbsey. The blonde six-year-old raced into the house while her twin brother Freddie held the collar of a large, furry animal on their front lawn.

Bert, twelve, came running, followed by his dark-haired twin, Nan.

"Where's the new dog?" asked Bert, hurrying outside.

"Here. Oh, he's so strong!" Freddie spoke up. "See how he's tugging to get away?"

"Freddie! Let him go!" Bert shouted. "That's no dog, it's a wolf!"

Freddie obeyed and ran back, while Flossie, frightened, clung to her sister Nan.

"What shall we do, Bert?" asked Nan. Then she shouted in relief. "Here comes Daddy!"

Mr. Bobbsey drove up in his car, parked in the driveway, and stepped out. He was a tall, athletic man with a handsome face. Seeing his children's looks of fear, he said, "That wolf won't hurt anyone. He's a pet."

"A pet?" Freddie said.

"That's right," his father replied, walking over to them. "He's Lobo. Here comes his master now."

Around the corner strode a stocky, red-haired man dressed in a plaid sport shirt, blue jeans, and boots. He wore a red cap. Instantly the wolf ran to his master. Then the animal sat back on his haunches and looked up expectantly as introductions were made.

"Children," said Mr. Bobbsey, "this is Mike Quinn from the Province of Ontario in Canada. I let him and Lobo off a few blocks from here so Lobo could run a bit."

"And he came right to our house!" Flossie said gleefully. "He likes us."

As the little girl patted the wolf, Bert asked politely, "How did you come to Lakeport, Mr. Quinn?"

"I have a pilot friend who was flying his plane here," the Canadian replied. "He invited me to ride along."

"Mike manages a general store outside the town of Timmins," Mr. Bobbsey explained. "I own some land near there."

"So you decided to come to see us. How nice!" said Nan.

The red-haired man exchanged a look with Mr. Bobbsey. "I'm afraid my visit means trouble," he said. "I've brought a mystery with me."

"A mystery!" the twins exclaimed. "What is it?"

Mike patted his pocket. "It's in here. I'll tell you about it later." Then he added, "Would you like to see some of Lobo's tricks?"

"Yes!"

Mike took off his peaked, red cap and tossed it over his shoulder. The wolf ran to it, picked it up in his teeth, and carried the cap back to his master. The children clapped loudly.

Quickly Lobo rolled over on command, then threw back his head in a howling song. Finally he walked on his hind legs toward Flossie.

She held out her arms to him and cried, "Lobo, you're wonderful!"

"He's great!" Freddie agreed. Mike Quinn snapped a leash onto Lobo's collar, and they all walked up to the house.

Now Mrs. Bobbsey, a slender, pretty woman, came onto the porch and greeted their visitor. While her husband showed Mike to the guest room, the children led Lobo out to the kitchen.

Bert pushed open the door and the wolf bounded into the room. A stout colored woman who was standing by the stove screamed in fright. "What you got there, Bert Bobbsey?" she yelled. "Get it right out of my kitchen!"

"He won't hurt you, Dinah," Bert explained.

Dinah Johnson and her husband had lived with the Bobbseys as long as the children could remember. Dinah helped Mrs. Bobbsey with the housework while Sam worked in Mr. Bobbsey's lumberyard on the shore of Lake Metoka. They roomed on the third floor of the house.

Dinah shook her head in despair. "My goodness! I don't know what you children are going to bring in here next!"

"We'll put Lobo on the back porch," Nan said. "It's nice and cool there."

"He won't bother you," Flossie promised.

"Good 'nuff." Dinah managed a smile. "Just don't let him loose in here! And be sure nobody goes in my tomato patch," she added. "I got four big ripe ones I'm goin' to pick in a little while. We're havin' a special dish for supper—tomato surprise."

"Don't worry, Dinah," Nan said as they went out the door.

Bert grinned as he secured Lobo to the railing on the back porch. Dinah did scold about things, but she was always ready to help the children when they needed her.

"Flossie and I'll stay here and watch Lobo," said Freddie. Bert and Nan went back into the house, eager to join their visitor.

"Maybe Lobo's hungry," Freddie said. "I'll

ask Dinah for some doggie biscuits." In a few minutes he returned with three.

"We'll each give him half of one," he said and held the treat out to the wolf.

Lobo sniffed at the biscuit, then took it carefully in his mouth. In a twinkling he had swallowed it. A moment later Flossie's half was gone, too. Lobo looked longingly at the two biscuits Freddie was holding.

"He's still hungry," said Flossie with a sigh and begged Freddie to give the others to Lobo. Freddie did as his twin suggested.

The wolf rubbed his head against Flossie. "He's so tame!" she said. "I'll bet we could even ride him."

Freddie's eyes lit up. "That's a keen idea! Come on, Flossie, you can go first."

Quickly Freddie untied Lobo and led him into the yard.

Giggling, Flossie climbed onto the animal's back. The wolf stood still, then suddenly pricked up his ears. He stared at the tomato patch at the back of the yard. Out hopped a small rabbit.

Like a shot the wolf streaked toward the bunny. Flossie screeched and grabbed the fur around Lobo's neck.

"Hang on!" shouted Freddie, trying to catch the wolf as it chased the darting rabbit.

"Help!" cried Flossie

Suddenly the bunny hopped over the low fence back into Dinah's tomato patch and Lobo raced after him.

"Help!" cried Flossie as she flew over the wolf's head. She landed among the ripe tomatoes.

"Are you hurt?" Freddie cried as he ran up to her.

Flossie's lip trembled. "No, but I'm all squishy." She held up her hands which were wet with smashed tomatoes. "I'm sitting on one, too."

"What happened?" called Bert as he and Nan came running out of the house. Dinah was right behind them.

"Didn't I tell you children to keep out of that tomato patch?" she asked.

"I didn't mean to come in," quavered Flossie as Nan helped her little sister over the fence.

Freddie explained what had happened. "We're sorry," he added.

Dinah took Flossie's hand and said kindly, "Well, come along and get cleaned up." She looked at Flossie's dress and shook her head. "Child, you are one big tomato surprise!"

In spite of herself, Flossie had to giggle. Just then Lobo came trotting back and Bert tied him on the porch again.

"You'd better come in the house with us, Freddie," said Nan.

Fifteen minutes later when Flossie entered the living room with a fresh dress on, Nan said, "Come hear about Cedar Camp!"

"And Mr. Choochoo!" Freddie added.

Seeing Flossie's bewildered look, Mr. Bobbsey explained that there was a log cabin on his land in Ontario, which was called Cedar Camp. An Indian woodsman named Tommy Cheechoo lived there most of the year.

"Tommy is a Cree Indian," Mrs. Bobbsey added. "He came down to the Timmins area from his home in Moose Factory."

"Moose Factory!" Freddie exclaimed in excitement. "Do they make mooses there?"

As the grownups laughed, Mr. Bobbsey told the children that many years before, a group of Englishmen had come to Canada and established the Hudson's Bay Company to buy fur skins from the Indian trappers. The managers of the stations from which the furs were shipped were called factors.

"And so the stations are still called factories. It has nothing to do with the common meaning of factory."

"Oh!" Freddie sounded disappointed.

"Where is Moose Factory?" Bert wanted to know.

"At the mouth of the Moose River which runs into James Bay, which in turn empties into Hudson Bay," Mike answered.

"That's way up north," Bert said. "We've studied that part of Canada in geography." He exchanged looks with Nan. Both were burning with curiosity to know what had brought the visitor to Lakeport.

"Mr. Quinn," Nan said politely, "when are you going to tell us about the mystery in your pocket?"

The red-haired man looked at the twins' eager faces and smiled. "I've had such a good time talking I forgot all about it."

"Do you know what it is, Daddy?" Freddie put in.

"No. Only that Mike said he had an urgent message for me."

"Yes, I have," his friend said. "Tommy Cheechoo is very worried about something and asked me to give you this."

Mike reached into his pocket and pulled out a thin piece of wood shaving, which he passed to Mr. Bobbsey. The children could see crude printing on it.

"What does it say?" Nan asked eagerly.

Mr. Bobbsey looked puzzled as he read the message aloud:

"BEWARE FOUR-
WINGED BLACKBIRD."

CHAPTER II

A FUNNY PIE

"A FOUR-winged blackbird!" Freddie echoed. "I didn't know blackbirds ever had four wings!"

Mr. Bobbsey looked as puzzled as the children. "What does Tommy mean, Mike?" he asked the Canadian.

Mike shook his head. "You know Tommy doesn't speak much English. He just said he wanted you to have this message as soon as I could get it to you. He seemed mighty upset about something."

"Poor Mr. Choochoo!" Flossie piped up. "Can't you help him, Daddy?"

"I'd like to, Flossie," her father agreed. "If I only knew what he meant by a four-winged blackbird!"

"I wish we could solve the mystery," Nan said wistfully. The Bobbsey twins loved mysteries and had solved several. On a VISIT TO THE GREAT WEST they had found some missing cattle and also had located a runaway cowboy.

"If we went to Canada we could work on the case." Bert gave his father a meaningful look.

At that moment the sound of loud barking came from the backyard. When it kept up, Bert jumped from his chair. "Something's the matter with Snap!" He ran from the room followed by his brother and sisters.

They dashed through the kitchen and out to the back porch. Snap was the Bobbseys' shaggy white dog. He had once belonged to a circus. Now he was circling Lobo, who had broken away from the porch railing and stood in the middle of the yard. Snap walked around the wolf, carefully keeping his distance and barking furiously.

Snoop, the Bobbseys' black cat, was perched on the garage roof, his back arched and his fur standing on end.

"Snap! Snoop!" Bert called. "Be quiet! Lobo won't hurt you!"

"Better put the wolf in the garage, Bert," Mr. Bobbsey suggested. "Our pets aren't going to be happy with him around!"

Nan held Snap while Bert led Lobo away and tied him securely inside the garage. When the wolf was out of sight, Snap stopped barking and Snoop came down from the roof. The cat rubbed against Freddie's legs as if nothing had happened.

"You'll like Lobo when you know him better," Freddie assured his pet.

At the supper table there was more discussion of Tommy Cheechoo's strange message, but no one could find any explanation for it. Mike told Mr. Bobbsey that Tommy had been doing his usual work of felling trees for the lumber companies. He had not seemed to be in any trouble.

After supper Nellie Parks, Nan's slender, pretty friend, and several other neighborhood children gathered on the Bobbseys' front lawn for a ball game.

Freddie and Flossie told Nellie about the strange warning from Indian Tommy. "Did you ever see a four-winged blackbird?" Flossie asked her seriously.

Nellie looked doubtful. "I don't believe there is such a thing," she replied.

Standing nearby was Danny Rugg, a big boy of Bert's age. Danny often played mean tricks on other children, especially younger ones. Having overheard the conversation, he snickered and walked off, whistling.

The next morning while the small twins were weeding the flower beds in front of the house, Danny came along. Seeing Flossie and Freddie alone, he walked up to them.

"I heard you talking about a four-winged blackbird last night," he began. "Haven't you really ever seen one?"

Freddie straightened up. "There isn't a bird like that," he said.

"Have you seen one, Danny?" Flossie asked.

"Sure! There's one in those woods at the end of our street. I'm surprised you Bobbseys haven't seen it. You always know everything!"

"Will you show us?" Flossie pleaded.

"We-ell." Danny appeared to consider the matter. "Okay. I'll take you there now."

"Let's wait till Bert and Nan come back from the store," Freddie suggested. "They can go too."

Danny started off. "If you want me to show you the bird, it'll have to be now. I'll be too busy later!"

"Come on, Freddie," Flossie begged. "I want to see the blackbird!"

"All right." Freddie followed Danny and Flossie out of the yard and down the street. Minutes later they entered the woods.

"He usually stays in one tree," Danny told the small twins. "It's over this way." They walked deeper and deeper into the woods.

Finally Danny stopped in front of a particularly tall oak tree and pointed to the topmost branches. "The four-winged blackbird lives up there," he said. "If you watch carefully, you'll see him."

Freddie and Flossie moved to the foot of the big oak. With their hands clasped behind them they stood, peering up into the leafy branches. A second later Danny tiptoed away softly.

When Bert and Nan returned from their errand they looked around the yard where they had left their young brother and sister. Little piles of weeds lay beside the flower beds, but there was no sign of the small twins.

"Dinah, have you seen Freddie and Flossie?" Nan asked, running into the kitchen where the cook was busy mixing batter.

"They were out front a little while ago. I heard 'em fussin' about who was pullin' the most weeds." Dinah chuckled.

Nan shrugged. "Perhaps they're with Mother."

"No. Your mother and father are drivin' that Mr. Quinn around town. Freddie and Flossie didn't go with them." Dinah was beginning to sound worried. "Maybe they went down to Susie Larker's house." Susie was Flossie's best friend.

Several telephone calls failed to locate the small twins. Bert and Nan were just starting out to search the neighborhood when their parents drove up with Mike Quinn.

"Maybe Lobo can find them," Mike suggested when he heard of the missing children. "Wolves are good trackers."

"I'm sure the twins haven't gone far away," Mrs. Bobbsey said, "but perhaps Lobo can find them faster than we can."

"Let's try it!" Bert dashed off to the garage and soon returned with the wolf on his leash.

Nan ran upstairs and brought down an old pair of Freddie's sneakers. She held them out to the wolf, who sniffed them curiously.

"Find Freddie!" Mike ordered. He led the wolf along the flower beds, where the small twins had been working, then let him smell the sneakers once more. "Go on, find Freddie and Flossie!" he urged.

Lobo ran up and down the flower beds, then suddenly headed for the street. Bert still held the leash and was pulled rapidly along. Nan and Mike ran after them. Occasionally Lobo paused to sniff at the ground, then trotted on, his bushy tail held straight out.

"He's making for the woods!" Nan exclaimed. "I hope Freddie and Flossie aren't lost in there!"

Reaching the trees, the wolf slowed his pace. He walked carefully, his nose to the ground. The others followed, looking in every direction.

Suddenly Nan cried out, "I see them!" She ran off among the trees.

Freddie and Flossie turned in surprise as Nan came up to them. "We're watching for the four-winged blackbird," Flossie told her proudly. "Danny says there's one in this tree!"

"He does, does he?" Bert said grimly. "Danny is just playing another of his tricks on you two.

He knows there's no bird with four wings!"

Freddie and Flossie looked disappointed but cheered up at the sight of the wolf. "Are you taking Lobo for a walk?" Freddie inquired.

"He's the one who found you," Nan told him. Freddie and Flossie were delighted and hugged the animal.

Bert and Nan walked together on the way home. "I wish we could play a trick on Danny to get even," Bert mused.

"We'll think of something," Nan assured him.

Back home they found Dinah making cherry tarts for luncheon. Nan looked at Bert, a twinkle in her eye. "I have an idea!"

"What is it?"

"Let's make Danny a blackbird pie!"

"Great, but how'll we do it?"

Nan ran up to her desk and came back with a large piece of black paper and a pair of scissors. She explained her scheme and soon the two were cutting tiny figures of birds from the paper.

"Will you help us, Dinah?" Nan asked.

"I sure will, honey," Dinah replied. "That Danny Rugg needs to be taught a lesson!" She chuckled as Nan told her the plan.

When the bird figures were finished, Dinah cut out pie dough enough for two small crusts. The paper birds were placed between them.

"Let's put in a little pepper for good measure," Bert suggested. He picked up the pepper mill and ground out a generous layer. Then Dinah put on the top crust and popped the pie into the oven to brown.

That afternoon Bert and Nan took up their watch on the front porch. It was not long before Danny, whose hands were deep in his pockets, came strolling up the street.

"Hi, Danny!" Bert called.

The bully stopped and looked nervously up at the porch.

"That was a pretty funny trick you played on Freddie and Flossie this morning," Bert went on. "We found them still looking up into that tree."

Danny grinned uncertainly.

"Dinah just made some nice little pies. Come on up and have one," Nan urged.

Danny was very fond of pie and could not resist the invitation. He came up onto the porch and took the pie which Bert offered.

"Gee, thanks," he said. "It looks good!" He bit into the flaky crust. As his teeth met the crisp paper and the pepper went up his nose, Danny yelled, then began to sneeze.

"Wh—wh—what? *A-choo!*" He stopped, unable to speak.

Grinning, Bert and Nan began to sing:
"Four-winged blackbirds
Baked in a pie!"
Danny stared at the tiny, paper blackbirds

"A-CHOO!"

and turned crimson. "You two think you're smart!" he blurted. "I didn't hurt Freddie and Flossie. If they're dumb enough to think birds have four wings, it's not my fault!" Still muttering, he fled down the steps and out to the street.

Freddie and Flossie, who had been watching from inside the house, ran out giggling. "Danny didn't like his pie, did he?" Freddie chortled.

At supper that evening Mr. Bobbsey told the children that Mike's pilot friend was going to pick him up at the Lakeport Airport that evening. The family drove out to see their new friend and his pet off for home. Mike shook hands with each one and thanked Mrs. Bobbsey for her hospitality.

He smiled broadly at Mr. Bobbsey. "I'll be seeing you soon."

Flossie ran to her father. "Daddy, you have your secret look! What is it?"

Mr. Bobbsey laughed. "Can't you guess? We're all going to Canada!"

CHAPTER III

OFF TO CANADA

"TO Cedar Camp?" Flossie jumped up and down in excitement. "To find the four-winged blackbird?"

Mr. Bobbsey patted Flossie's curly head. "That's right. I'm still puzzled about the blackbird, my little fat fairy," he said with a smile. "I want to find out what Tommy Cheechoo's warning means."

The children's father had special nicknames for the younger twins. He called Flossie his little fat fairy because she was inclined to be chubby. He had named Freddie his little fat fireman, because Freddie loved to play with his toy fire engine. He declared he was going to be a fireman some day.

Now Freddie beamed. "Hooray! We're going to Canada and meet an Indian!"

"And we can play with Lobo some more," Flossie spoke up.

After Mike Quinn and his pilot friend had taken off, Mr. Bobbsey drove toward home.

"Besides seeing Tommy, I have some business to take up with a lumberman in Timmins," he told his family. "This will be a good opportunity for you children to see a bit of Canada."

"And Mr. Choochoo!" Flossie added with a giggle.

The next few days were busy ones as preparations for the trip were made. Finally the big day came and the Bobbseys left on an early morning flight for Kennedy Airport in New York.

After checking in at the Canadian Airlines counter there, Mr. Bobbsey told his family that they had almost an hour before taking off for Toronto. "That's where we change planes for Timmins," he added.

Mrs. Bobbsey agreed to go with the younger twins who were eager to try one of the picture-taking booths they had heard about from their friends.

"May Nan and I go outside?" Bert asked his father. "We'd like to look at some of the new airline terminal buildings."

"Very well," their father replied. "But please watch the time."

"We will," the twins promised.

Out in the street, Nan and Bert admired the new modern buildings. Finding they had walked a fair distance on their inspection tour, they stopped at the Pan American building to rest on one of the comfortable benches. Watching the passengers, they became amused by some children playing nearby.

"Where do you think they come from?" Bert whispered to his sister. "They're speaking a foreign language."

"They look Scandinavian—blond and blue-eyed," Nan replied. "Their mother seems upset. I wonder why."

Just then one of the children gave a hearty pitch to his rubber ball and it rolled out of reach, heading toward Bert. He put out his hand quickly to stop it. Realizing the child might be frightened to take the ball from a stranger, Bert walked over and handed it to his mother.

"Oh, thank you," the attractive woman said. "We have had much difficulty today. The children would have cried if we had lost one more thing."

"I'm sorry," Bert said politely. "Did you lose something valuable?"

"Our luggage is gone!" the woman explained. "We have just arrived from Sweden and have only the things we carried with us; no clothes, no food for the baby!"

"I'm sure the airline will find your luggage," Bert said, hoping he sounded encouraging.

"I'm afraid they have forgotten me," the woman said, close to tears. "With four children, especially my baby son, I can't stand at the counter and wait for news."

"If you will let us, my sister and I would be glad to stay with the children while you check about your baggage," Bert offered.

"Just the baby, thank you," said the woman, handing him the infant. She looked relieved as she hurried off with her other children.

Nan came over quickly. As Bert told her the problem, the dark-haired girl gently rocked the baby in her arms. The child slept briefly, but then started to cry. The twins made every effort to quiet him.

"Bert, it's time we were getting back. What do you think is keeping the woman?"

"I'll go find her and explain we just can't wait any longer," Bert declared firmly as he walked off.

It seemed to Nan as if Bert had been gone a very long time. Hard as she tried, she could not quiet the screaming baby. "Maybe the poor thing is hungry," Nan thought. "Oh, I do wish Bert would hurry."

Finally, she saw her twin crossing the room with a puzzled look on his face.

"I couldn't find the mother anywhere," he said worriedly. "Can't we do something to quiet him?" he added, looking down at the wailing baby. "Everyone is staring at us."

"You hold him while I get some milk," Nan

"You hold him!"

said, thrusting the baby into her brother's arms and taking off before he could object.

The embarrassed, red-faced boy held the screaming, equally red-faced baby like a package of exploding firecrackers.

Nan was relieved to locate a machine which poured milk into a paper cup. Hurrying back across the room, she carefully watched the cup to be certain she would not spill its contents.

At that moment she saw the missing mother and children hastening toward Bert and his howling charge.

"Thank goodness," Nan heard the woman apologizing to Bert for having been gone so long. "They have located our luggage. I am so happy," she said, taking the baby who immediately went to sleep.

"Thank you ever so much," the woman added to the twins, who quickly said good-by and ran as fast as they could to rejoin their family.

"Where have you been?" said Mr. Bobbsey, who was pacing by the door. Not waiting for an answer, he hurried the children along, explaining that the plane was being held for them.

Once aboard, the older twins told their parents of their baby-sitting adventure. Though they had caused some anxious moments, Mr. and Mrs. Bobbsey and Flossie and Freddie laughed heartily at the thought of Bert holding a shrieking baby.

Late that afternoon, the big plane set down at the Toronto Airport. After a brief wait, the Bobbseys boarded a smaller aircraft which was soon in the air heading for Timmins. They could see nothing but a black expanse of forest below. The plane came down at a small airport, seemingly in the middle of nowhere.

"Everybody off!" Mr. Bobbsey sang out.

"There's nothing out there," Nan spoke up.

Mr. Bobbsey smiled. "Mike and a car are somewhere out there—I hope."

"I think Canada is spooky," observed Flossie as they walked from the plane to the low, flat building that served as an air terminal.

Mike's familiar red hair was soon spotted and the twins waved a hearty greeting to their Canadian friend.

"Look!" Flossie cried. "Mike brought Lobo with him!"

The sight of his friends from Lakeport was too much for the friendly wolf. He gave such a strong pull at his leash that the rope was yanked from the hand of his surprised master. Like a bullet, the animal shot through the crowd toward the new arrivals. Eagerly he leaped up on Freddie, almost knocking the small boy down. Jumping from one twin to the next, he licked their hands and faces.

Mike laughed. "Howdy, folks. Well, you can't say you aren't welcome," he said, smiling, and stooped to pick up the dragging leash. "Now that the official greeting is finished," he added, "let's go find your luggage."

While waiting for their suitcases to be unloaded from the plane, Mike chatted with the twins' parents. The children played happily with Lobo.

Mike picked up most of their luggage as it was placed on the counter. With a rousing cry, "Cedar Camp, here we come!" he led the way to his car. Mr. Bobbsey and Bert carried the remaining suitcases and Lobo helped too, by carrying Nan's small airline bag between his teeth.

They drove through blackness for some distance but soon spotted lights ahead. Mike announced they were approaching Timmins.

"Where did everyone come from?" Nan asked in astonishment as they drove through the main street. Indeed, many of the stores were still open and crowds of people were milling about.

"Timmins is very crowded at the present time," Mike explained. "We have had some new, rich mineral strikes and the town is full of prospectors."

"Golly, have all these people discovered gold?" Freddie asked.

"Not quite, young man," the kindly Canadian replied. "But you can bet they all hope to strike it rich."

"Is there really enough gold to make all these people rich?" Flossie inquired.

"No, and unfortunately, that is the problem. People get greedy and want more and more gold for themselves," Mike explained.

"Well, if I find any gold, I'll share it with Freddie," Flossie declared, and everyone smiled.

Soon Timmins had been left behind and tall pines rose on both sides of the road. The trees grew thicker until finally Mike pulled off into a clearing and stopped. *Cedar Camp,* the sign read.

"We have to walk in from here," Mike explained. "Tommy is expecting you, and I am certain you will find the cabin shipshape."

The men carried the suitcases and Mike led the way along a narrow trail. Finally the dark shape of a cabin loomed ahead. Mr. Bobbsey pounded loudly on the door.

"Tommy!" he called. "Tommy!"

There was no answer.

CHAPTER IV

CABIN INTRUDER

THE twins looked at one another. Would they have to sleep in the woods?

Mr. Bobbsey and Mike continued to knock and call Tommy Cheechoo's name, but not a sound was heard from inside the log cabin.

Trying the door, Mike found it to be unlocked, pushed it open, and went inside. As the Bobbseys waited, a flickering light suddenly shone. Mike came to the door, an oil lamp in his hand.

"Step right in, folks," he called. "Your home-away-from-home awaits you."

The twins laughed as they entered the cabin which was now brightened by several oil lamps which Mike was lighting.

"What do you suppose has happened to Tommy?" Mrs. Bobbsey inquired worriedly.

"He's probably out hunting or cutting line,

and is too far away to come back tonight," Mr. Bobbsey suggested.

"What's cutting line?" Bert asked.

"Cutting a path through the woods with a hand ax," his father explained. "Sometimes Tommy works for the mining companies. He cuts a trail three or four feet wide from the road to the site of the company's claim. The engineers and miners use the path to get to work."

"Wait a minute!" Mike exclaimed, holding open the door to a wide closet. "It seems as if Tommy is not working. Here's his gun and ax. He can't do much without these."

Mike turned away from the closet and looked around the room. "It doesn't appear as if anyone had been here to prepare for your arrival. The extra bedding I brought is still on the bench, and I don't see much food on the shelves."

Mr. Bobbsey realized their friend was embarrassed as well as concerned. "Don't worry. We'll get along. I guess Tommy will be back tomorrow."

Mike called Lobo and said they must leave now. "I'll be over first thing in the morning with some food for breakfast," he promised as he left.

The twins examined the cabin curiously. It was divided into two large rooms with a shed at the rear. An oil stove, evidently used for cooking, stood in a corner of the front room. Above it was a shelf of groceries. In the center of the room was a large table made of cedar logs. The benches along two sides were also cedar.

Tommy's bed stood in another corner. It was made of boughs covered by several blankets. Against each wall were two low bunks.

"You can look around in the morning, children," Mrs. Bobbsey said briskly. "I think it's time we all got some sleep!"

Mr. Bobbsey and the boys stayed in the main room while Mrs. Bobbsey and the girls went into the other one.

"I'll bet we like Mr. Choochoo," Flossie declared, as she climbed into her bunk.

"Cheechoo, honey," said Nan sleepily and Flossie repeated the name correctly.

The Bobbseys were surprised how tired they were and soon the only sound to be heard was the wind blowing through the trees. Freddie, however, was not entirely ready for sleep. A slit in the logs beside his bunk had been stuffed with material to keep out the cold. By pulling away the cloth, and with the help of a bright moon, he had a fine view of the woods.

"I'd better keep a look-out for Indians," he thought, but soon sleep overcame the young watchman.

When the children awoke the next morning, the aroma of frying bacon and pancakes filled the air.

"Mmm!" Flossie cried. "That surely smells

yummy!" She and Nan hurriedly put on slacks and sweaters, then ran out to find Mike cooking at the oil stove.

"I thought you might enjoy a North Woods breakfast," he said cheerfully as he served helping after helping of the good pancakes and Canadian bacon to the hungry family.

"I like Cedar Camp!" declared Freddie as he poured more maple syrup over his stack of cakes.

After the hearty meal was finished, Mike offered to drive them all to town. Mrs. Bobbsey said she and the young twins would shop for supplies.

"While they are doing the buying, I'll take the rest of you sightseeing," he offered.

Mike dropped the shoppers at his General Store, then gave the others a tour of Mr. Bobbsey's timberland, which covered many acres around Cedar Camp. He drove them down a bumpy, dirt road between tall spruce and firs.

"Let's stop, Mike, and have a look around," Mr. Bobbsey suggested.

While the two men were examining trees, Bert spotted a trampled section of ground. In the center was a deep round hole about two inches in diameter. Some distance away Nan found another. Bert called the men over to see.

Mike gave a low whistle. "This hole was

made by a drill," he said. "Somebody's been prospecting here."

"Maybe this is what Tommy Cheechoo's warning is about," Nan said, "but what has it got to do with a four-winged blackbird?"

Bert shook his head, puzzled. "Search me!" Suddenly he knelt beside the hole and picked up something.

"Did you find a clue?" Nan asked.

"Oh boy, did I!" exclaimed her excited twin. "See this!" Bert was holding a shiny piece of yellowish metal in his hand.

"Gold!" Nan cried.

Hearing the excitement, Mike and Mr. Bobbsey came over to investigate. "Let me see," Mike suggested and Bert handed him the rock.

"I hate to disappoint you," Mike said, smiling. "This mineral is pyrite, often referred to as fool's gold. It looks like the real thing and is often found with it, but unfortunately, is not valuable."

"Oh," Bert responded.

"Don't be sad, young man," the kindly Canadian said. "There are people around here who have been hoping for years to discover gold."

"I guess I can't really expect to strike it rich in less than twenty-four hours, can I?" Bert said good-naturedly.

Meanwhile, Mrs. Bobbsey was going over her

long shopping list with a clerk in the store. Freddie and Flossie, fascinated by the variety of goods for sale, as well as the unusual appearance of the customers, were wandering about.

"Look, Freddie," said his sister, trying not to laugh. "How can that one little man eat all those groceries?" A very short, stocky miner was buying large sacks of flour, sugar, bacon, and other goods he would need on a long camping trip.

"He must not go to market so often as Dinah," Freddie suggested.

Leaving his sister looking at dresses which had been made from gaily printed flour sacks, he went over to a long row of glass jars filled with different colored candy sticks.

"Would you like a red one, young man?" the elderly man asked. He wore a leather jacket and high boots. Freddie quickly decided he must be a real prospector—he had a long, gray matted beard.

Freddie accepted the candy and listened as the man finished ordering the large supply of food. "Do you eat all of that yourself?" Freddie asked as he happily sucked on the candy.

"Oh, yes," said the man, smiling. "But not all at once. This supply will have to last me for several weeks. There are no stores out in the bush."

The little boy looked puzzled. "The bush?"

"That's what we call the wilderness," explained the prospector. "I live there when I'm searching for gold, I do."

"Have you found any gold?" the little boy asked.

"Once I sure did," the prospector said, looking off into space. "Would you like to hear 'bout it?"

"Oh, yes," Freddie said eagerly as he climbed onto a nearby wooden barrel.

"Well, it's a sad story, son," the miner commenced, delighted to have such an interested audience. "I was just a young fella when I first came up here determined to strike it rich. I got me a supply of food and water, some prospectin' equipment, a sleepin' bag and headed down river. Days I spent in the hot sun panning for gold."

"Panning?" interrupted Freddie. "What does that mean?"

"My, young fella, you really are a stranger to these parts," the prospector commented. "Panning is finding gold by using a shallow pan and washing dirt. Gold is heavy and will sink to the bottom of the pan while the gravel and pebbles are on top and can be easily removed.

"Good fortune, I did have," the old man continued. "I found so much gold, I kept working, going for days without food or water. Finally, I had exhausted the area and decided to return to town and claim my wealth. The last night as I was going to sleep, I saw them. Indians!"

By this time, Freddie had put down the candy and was sitting on the very edge of the wooden barrel.

"Yep," the prospector went on, "so many Indians you cannot imagine, creeping along the riverbank toward my little camp. Quickly, I ran into the woods and hid under some old logs. Escape, I did, thank goodness. But the gold— gone. Weeks of work, gone in a flash."

Suddenly loud screams interrupted the prospector's story.

"Indians!" cried Freddie, leaping off his perch and heading for the door.

But there were no Indian men. Flossie had been watching two Indian women braiding rugs in a corner of the store. Stepping back to admire a rug, she had knocked over a pan of red dye. The gooey mass had splattered onto Flossie's shoes and one of the woman's rugs. The Indian woman had screamed in anger at the poor child. "My rug, my rug, ruined!"

Flossie looked at the red mess and started to cry. Hearing the commotion, Mrs. Bobbsey quickly came to Flossie's assistance. The Indian woman quieted when Mrs. Bobbsey offered to pay for the damage.

"I think it's time we went home," Mrs. Bobb-

"Indians!" cried Freddie

sey declared, looking at her daughter's red shoes and her son's sticky red face. Mike soon arrived with Bert and Nan. Right behind them came Mr. Bobbsey in a brown station wagon.

"I knew we'd need a car so I rented this," he said as the rest of the family got in with him.

Both drivers headed back to Cedar Camp. They parked in the roadside clearing and everyone helped carry the groceries up the path to the cabin.

"Boy, am I hungry," Bert declared, opening the door for his mother.

As Mrs. Bobbsey stepped inside she stopped in dismay. The floor was covered with muddy footprints, suitcases had been opened, clothing was scattered about the room.

"Someone has been here while we were gone!" Nan exclaimed.

CHAPTER V

GLOWING EYES

WHO, was the question in everyone's mind—who had been searching in the cabin?

"What could he be looking for?" Mrs. Bobbsey asked.

"Maybe Mr. Cheechoo was here," Flossie suggested.

"I am certain Tommy was not responsible for this," Mike declared. He examined the muddy footprints. "These are all the same size and boot-sole pattern. Only one man must have been here. Let's check, Dick, to see if anything is missing." After a careful search, Mr. Bobbsey announced nothing had been taken.

"Whoever did this must have been looking for something special," said Bert.

"But what?" asked Nan.

Mr. Bobbsey frowned. "It's a mystery," he said.

"I wonder if our intruder is connected with the

mystery of the four-winged blackbird," said Bert.

"It's possible," said his father.

Mrs. Bobbsey sighed and looked around. "Such a mess!" she declared. "We never can eat until the place is cleaned up."

"I have an idea!" Mike said cheerfully. "Suppose you Bobbseys be my guests at lunch in town. I usually eat my main meal at noon. After you've had some food, cleaning house won't seem so bad." He grinned.

The family agreed and everyone went back to Mike's car. Half an hour later they pulled up in front of a small restaurant in Timmins.

"At this place, Freddie," said Mike with a wink, "you can get rabbit soup, moose steak, and calves' foot jelly— Which do you want?"

The little boy looked worried. "Ca-can't you get anything that isn't made out of an animal like—like ice cream?"

"Oh, sure, we have prickly pear ice cream," Mike continued to tease.

After a sensible meal of chicken and apple pie, the Bobbseys returned to the cabin. Everyone pitched in and soon their rustic home was shipshape. Then Mrs. Bobbsey said, "We need some water for cooking and washing. Who'll get it for me?"

"I will," said Bert promptly and the others offered to help.

Carrying two buckets and a small pail, the children went to the old pump in the clearing beside the cabin. Bert and Nan took turns pumping the long handle while the young twins watched the water pour into the containers.

"Let me do it," Freddie begged. His brother allowed him to pump for a while.

"Now me!" said Flossie. As she worked, her face grew red.

She and Freddie carried the pail into the cabin while Bert and Nan followed with the buckets.

Mrs. Bobbsey thanked them. "You're real pioneers," she said with a smile. "Every drop of water they used had to be pumped or drawn out of a well."

"Or carried from a stream," Nan added.

Flossie wiped her face with her sleeve. "Being pioneers must have been hard work," she said.

The children played near the cabin the rest of the day. As the shadows began to lengthen, their thoughts returned to the mysterious intruder.

"Do you think he'll come back, Bert?" Freddie asked anxiously.

"I guess not," said his brother cheerfully. He patted the little boy's shoulder. "Don't worry about it."

But Bert could not help wondering if the intruder had found what he was looking for. If not, would he try again?

Just before bedtime Bert and his father went out for a stroll around the cabin. The stars were bright, but the encircling woods was black.

Suddenly there came a loud crack of a twig from the underbrush. Both Bobbseys stopped and listened. They could see nothing in the dark woods.

Quietly Mr. Bobbsey stepped toward the trees. Another crackling was heard.

"Sounds like something moved away," whispered Bert. "I'll get a flashlight."

He hastened into the cabin. Not wanting to alarm the others, he said nothing. He took the light from his suitcase and went out again. His father was gone!

As Bert stood still, listening, there came a soft *snap!* The boy stepped toward the sound. Just inside the edge of the woods stood Mr. Bobbsey! He snapped his fingers at Bert again and beckoned to him.

The boy slipped to his father's side and flicked on his light. Instantly there came another rustle of something moving away.

Bert turned the beam toward the noise. Two large green eyes glowed in the dark! Then a dark shape leaped over a bush and vanished among the trees.

Mr. Bobbsey chuckled. "Look son, it's only a deer!"

Bert grinned. "I thought it was the intruder

"Look, son, it's only a deer!"

coming back. What could he have been after, Dad?"

"I don't know," said Mr. Bobbsey. "But something strange is going on and we must keep our eyes and ears open."

Next morning Tommy Cheechoo still had not returned. "He must have had to go somewhere suddenly on personal business," said Mr. Bobbsey. "Maybe he'll turn up today."

After the twins had helped their mother with the breakfast dishes, Mr. Bobbsey suggested they go at once to visit his friend, Jim McLain.

"Who's he, Daddy?" asked Nan, "the lumberman you came to see?"

"No," her father said. "Jim is superintendent of the Aurora Gold Mine."

"Jeepers!" Freddie exclaimed. "A real gold mine! Can we go way down to the bottom with the miners?"

"I'll ask Jim," Mr. Bobbsey said.

Excited by the idea, the twins raced along the path ahead of their parents and piled into the station wagon. When they reached the mine, they immediately went up to the superintendent's office. His secretary ushered them into his private room. Mr. McLain, a tall, slender man with sandy hair and blue eyes, greeted them cordially.

"I'm sorry, Dick," the superintendent replied when asked if the twins could visit the mine.

"No one under eighteen is permitted to do that. You and Mary can go, though. A tour starts in a few minutes. While you're gone, I'd be glad to show the youngsters around up here."

The children were disappointed, but pleased for their parents. They waited in the comfortable chairs, while Mr. McLain took the couple to get outfitted for the tour.

When their mother and father returned, the twins stared in amazement, then began to laugh. Mrs. Bobbsey wore slacks and a blue denim jacket several sizes too big for her. A leather belt holding a battery case was around her waist. On her head was a round, yellow metal hat with a light in the front. Her eyes were covered with safety goggles. Completing the outfit were heavy boots and gloves. Mr. Bobbsey's clothes were similar.

"Wow!" exclaimed Freddie. "You look as if you're going to a Halloween party."

Mr. McLain smiled. "These are miners' working clothes and they're designed for safety. Come along," he added and led them through the hall into an enormous room with elevators at one end.

There the children watched their parents join a tour group and step into a huge car which disappeared into the ground. Mr. McLain then took the twins outside for a walk around the buildings.

"Does anyone ever steal gold from your mine?" Nan inquired.

"Yes, they do," he replied. "One of our greatest problems is high-graders."

"What are they?" asked Bert.

"Miners who work in the high-grade ore, where most of the gold is found. They take pieces of the ore, go off by themselves in a tunnel, crush the rock and extract the precious metal. A small amount of pure gold will bring a high price."

"Can't you catch them?" Bert asked.

"Not very often. We can't figure out how they get the gold off the premises. Come with me, I'll show you how we check on the miners."

The superintendent led the children into a big room. Suspended on pulleys from the high ceiling were hundreds of garments—miners' overalls, boots, caps.

"Look!" Flossie giggled as she pointed out a suit of long underwear.

"When the miners come to the surface," the superintendent said, "they leave their clothes here, shower, and file past a metal detector before they reach the room where their own clothing is kept. Therefore, we cannot understand how they manage to get the stolen gold out of the building."

"That is a puzzle," Bert agreed. "Perhaps we

can solve it for you. We like to work on mysteries."

"I certainly would be grateful if you could," the kindly man replied. "Now suppose we go see some of the exhibits."

He led the way to the hall where they found glass cases with models of the mine in them. "You can see here that there are many levels down inside," said Mr. McLain, "and miners dig in all of them." He pointed out models of the supply rooms and the huge machinery which worked the elevators from deep in the earth.

"These models are like doll houses," remarked Nan, "because you can see into them."

"There are even teeny men in the tunnels," said Flossie.

"And little trains of open cars to carry the ore," added Freddie.

Seeing how interested the twins were, Mr. McLain asked if they could look around by themselves. The children assured Mr. McLain that they would wait near there for their parents. The superintendent said good-by then and returned to his office.

Flossie, spying some brilliant flowers on a wide expanse of lawn, asked her sister if they could go out and play on the grass. Nan said yes, provided they stay close to the main door. The boys continued examining the displays.

"Here they come," Freddie declared as the tourists, with muddy boots, walked into the hall from the big elevator room. A group of miners entered right behind them and headed for the place where they were to leave their clothes.

"There's Mother," Freddie said, and darted across the hall. As Bert started to follow, a small, thin tourist with an ugly scar on his chin, came hurrying through the crowd. The next moment he collided with Bert.

"Why don't you watch where you're going!" he growled and hurried on.

"You all right, Bert?" Mr. Bobbsey inquired as he and Mrs. Bobbsey reached their son.

"Yes," he replied. "But I haven't any idea why that man was so annoyed. He would have bumped into one of the miners anyhow, the way he was headed."

That night, after the family had crawled into their beds, Freddie pulled out the brown cloth and watched the moonlit woods through his peephole. The shadows of the tall trees played tricks on his imagination and he saw bears and lions skulking there. "Maybe I will see an Indian," he thought to himself.

Becoming drowsy, he started to put the cloth back in its hole when he heard a rustling noise. Wide awake, he squinted through the opening. A small figure was creeping up to the cabin!

CHAPTER VI

DEVIL ROCK

"INDIANS!" thought Freddie. He jumped from his bunk and shook his brother, who was lying in the next one.

Bert awoke with a start. "What's the matter?"

"Indians!" whispered Freddie. "They're creeping up on us!"

"You were dreaming," said Bert. "Go back to bed."

"No," insisted Freddie. "I saw one. Look out the window."

"Okay," said Bert, getting up. "But be quiet. You'll wake Daddy." Mr. Bobbsey was sound asleep in a bunk across the cabin.

The boys tiptoed to the window beyond Bert's bunk. The clearing was empty!

"See," said the older boy. "Now go back to bed."

"I saw somebody, honest, Bert!"

"All right," his brother said patiently. "Let's take a look outside."

49

They put on slippers and robes. Then Bert quietly opened the door. Stepping onto the porch, they saw a dark figure slip around the end of the cabin.

Quickly Bert padded down the steps and rounded the corner. A boy was standing on tiptoes, peering through a window!

"Hey you!" said Bert.

Startled, the stranger ran. Bert sprinted and brought him down with a flying tackle.

Meanwhile Freddie had roused the whole family. Mr. Bobbsey came racing around the corner.

"What's going on?" he exclaimed. He separated the struggling boys and hauled the prowler to his feet.

"I caught him looking in the window," Bert explained, panting. The young stranger was trembling.

"Suppose we go inside and find out what this is all about," Mr. Bobbsey said, guiding the boy firmly, but kindly, into the cabin.

Nan was lighting the oil lamp on the table. In the soft glow the Bobbseys looked at the boy. He was slender with black hair and piercing black eyes. His skin was a deep tan.

"What's your name, young man?" Mr. Bobbsey asked.

"Little Moose," was the reply.

"An Indian!" Freddie exclaimed.

The boy nodded. "I am a Cree."

"How old are you?" Flossie piped up.

"Fourteen," he replied. Then squaring his shoulders, he said bravely, "Where is my friend, Tommy Cheechoo? You have not hurt him?"

"Of course not! We wouldn't hurt anybody," said Nan.

Mrs. Bobbsey patted the boy's shoulder. "Sit down," she said. "Let's have some hot chocolate."

While Nan followed her mother to the stove, the others took seats at the big cedar table. Mr. Bobbsey introduced the family to the boy and explained why they were at the cabin. At the mention of the four-winged blackbird, the Indian looked puzzled.

"Where do you live?" Freddie asked.

"In the woods," the Indian replied. "My grandmother has a cabin about a mile from here. I spend summers with her. My father, Big Moose, is a bush pilot," he added proudly. "He flies all over this country."

"I remember," said Mr. Bobbsey. "Your grandmother was living on this land when I bought it. I told her then she is welcome here."

"When did you last see Tommy Cheechoo?" Bert asked the boy.

"Four days ago. He promised to visit us yesterday, but he did not show up. I came here today and saw many people. Tonight I wanted to find out who you are and if you harmed Tommy."

"You didn't come into the cabin at anytime, did you?" asked Mr. Bobbsey.

"No," said Little Moose. "Why?"

Bert told him about the muddy tracks and upset suitcases. The Indian boy listened, troubled. But he smiled when Mrs. Bobbsey put cups of steaming hot chocolate on the table and a large plate of cookies. Shyly, he tried both.

"These are very good, thank you," he said.

"You should taste Dinah's cookies," Flossie said gaily, deciding she liked the boy. "They are super!"

As Little Moose made ready to leave, he apologized for having awakened the family. "I will come back in the morning with my father. He, too, is worried about Tommy."

"Why don't you have breakfast with us?" the twins' mother suggested. Little Moose accepted happily, then said good night and left.

Next morning Mrs. Bobbsey had just put a platter of steaming flapjacks on the table, when the boy and his father appeared.

Big Moose was a husky man with a shock of wiry, black hair. His gaze was direct, like his son's. Both were wearing colorful, cotton shirts.

"Tommy would not go off without ax or gun," the big Indian declared. "I am afraid something bad has happened to him."

"Maybe Lobo can find him," Freddie suggested.

"A good idea!" said Big Moose. "I know Mike and I'm sure he will let us borrow the wolf." He frowned. "But I must take out some prospectors in my plane, so I can't search for Tommy today."

"We'll go," said Freddie quickly and the other twins and Little Moose chimed in eagerly.

Mr. Bobbsey said he had a business appointment in town, but would stop first at the General Store and bring back the wolf.

"I thought you also had to pick up some papers from Mr. McLain at the mine," said Mrs. Bobbsey.

"Yes. I won't have much time," replied her husband, frowning. Quickly Bert offered to do the errand. Big Moose said he had his jeep and would drop him off at the mine.

"Thanks a lot, both of you," said Mr. Bobbsey. "Bert, you can take a taxi back here."

A few minutes later Bert was following the Indian pilot through the woods. After a half mile they came to a dirt road where a jeep was parked. The boy enjoyed the breezy ride to the gatehouse of the mine. Thanking Big Moose, he hopped out. Bert picked up a pass from the gatekeeper and hurried to the main building.

As he headed down the hall, a tour group passed, going toward the elevators. Bert stopped in surprise and gazed after the tourists. "That's funny," he said to himself. "I'm sure I saw the same man who bumped into me here yesterday. Why would he take the tour again today?"

Bert went into Mr. McLain's office, just as the superintendent opened his private door. He was surprised to see Bert, but guessed his errand. "Come on in," he said. "I'll give you the papers."

Meanwhile, Mike Quinn had arrived at the cabin. "I brought Lobo myself," he explained to Mrs. Bobbsey, "since Dick had so little time. I've been thinking," he added, "maybe you ought to keep Lobo here. He'd be protection for you."

"Like a watchdog," said Freddie.

"Only he'd be our watch *wolf*," Flossie added.

Mrs. Bobbsey smiled and thanked Mike. "That's an excellent idea."

As Flossie hugged the furry animal, Nan ran into the house and came back with a pair of hunting boots. "We can use these to track Tommy," she said, "if they belong to him. I found them in the closet."

"Yes, those are his," said Mike as Nan let the wolf sniff the shoes.

Moments later the animal trotted toward the woods. "He's picked up a trail!" exclaimed Nan. "Let's go!"

"If you run into any trouble," warned Mrs. Bobbsey, "come back at once for help."

"Lobo will protect them," said Mike.

The children promised to be careful, then raced off after the wolf. He ran straight along a path and in a little while came to a small clearing. The ground was humped up in three places with fresh earth.

"It looks like someone has been digging," said Nan.

Lobo cut back and forth across the open space, sniffing at the ground. Then he circled the edge. Finally he stopped and looked around.

"He's lost the scent," said Little Moose.

"Here's a footprint!" exclaimed Nan, pointing to a wide, deep track.

"And another!" added Flossie, showing them a still bigger print.

"Two men were here," said the Indian, "but one was not Tommy, or Lobo would recognize the scent."

"What do you suppose happened to him?" asked Nan, looking worried. "His trail just vanishes!"

"He couldn't fly through the air," declared Flossie.

Little Moose frowned. "It is very strange."

Spotting broken brush at the side of the clearing, the Indian motioned the others to follow.

"Someone walked this way," he said. "Maybe the two men who made the prints."

"Maybe they've seen Mr. Cheechoo," said Nan. "Let's try to find them."

Quietly the children and the wolf followed Little Moose, who pointed out the broken twigs and turned-over stones which showed him the trail. It was lost, at last, on a large stony patch.

Freddie sat down on a flat rock next to the wolf, whose tongue hung out. "I'm hot and thirsty," said the little boy. "So's Lobo."

"There's a spring over here," said the Indian, leading them to a clear stream which trickled from a split in a rock.

The children filled their cupped hands and drank while Lobo lapped at the little pool beneath.

"Now come," said Little Moose. "I will show you something very mysterious."

"What is it?" asked Nan.

"The Devil Rock—a big, stone face."

Once more he struck off through the woods and the Bobbseys followed. Suddenly Little Moose pointed ahead. "There's the Devil Rock!"

The Bobbseys ran up to the huge stone, which towered above their heads.

"Stand back here," their guide directed. "It is better seen from a distance."

The twins obeyed. They saw that the carved

"It's kind of scary," Flossie said

face had a grinning mouth and deep eyes with large, pointed eyebrows. On top of the head was a pair of devil's horns.

Flossie shivered. "It's kind of scary!"

"Who made it, Little Moose?" Nan asked.

The boy shrugged. "No one knows. It is said to be an ancient god worshipped by my ancestors."

For a minute the children stared in silence at the strange rock. Then Little Moose said, "There's an old abandoned mine over that way." He pointed ahead. "Sometime I'll show it to you, but I think we'd better go back now."

They started through the woods at a brisk pace. All at once the Indian motioned to them to halt. He stood still, listening intently.

In the silence they heard men's voices and a thudding noise.

"Someone is digging," he whispered. "Come quietly." He crept toward a heavy growth of brush.

As the others followed, Freddie stepped on a twig. *Snap!* Immediately the voices stopped and two burly men burst out of the bushes. One was blond with a red face.

The other had a shaggy, black beard and was carrying a spade. He started toward the children.

"What are you doing here?" he asked harshly.

CHAPTER VII

THE INDIAN PRINCESS

BEFORE the frightened children could speak, Lobo stiffened and growled.

The bearded man stopped in his tracks. His eyes slid to the wolf. With a sudden gasp, he stepped backward.

His companion stared, open-mouthed. "That's a wolf!" he exclaimed.

As he turned to run, a shiny object hanging around his neck glinted in the sun. The two men thrashed back through the bushes as Lobo leaped after them.

The children followed pell-mell and saw the men disappear among the trees. Little Moose sprinted after Lobo and caught him. He led the animal back to the twins, who were looking at a small hole in the ground.

"I'll bet those two men did the digging in the clearing," said Nan. "It was probably their tracks we saw."

The others agreed. "I wonder what they're burying," said Flossie.

"Maybe gold!" said her twin. "They could be mixed up with the high-graders at the mine."

"Perhaps," said Nan. "There's something else, too." She told about the big holes near the dirt road. "These men might be the trespassers who are prospecting."

"Maybe they hurt Mr. Cheechoo," said Flossie.

"They looked awfully mean," agreed Freddie with a shiver. "I hope they don't come back."

"We'd better make for camp," said Nan.

"We'll go a different way," said Little Moose, "—a short cut."

As the children hurried through the woods, Flossie spoke up. "What was that shiny thing the one man was wearing?"

"He had on a bolo tie," said Little Moose. "The ornament on the end was what we saw."

"But what made it shine?" Flossie persisted.

"It was a ball of pyrite," he said. Nan quickly explained to the young twins about fool's gold.

When the children arrived at the cabin, they found Mr. Bobbsey studying some papers at the table with his wife beside him. Bert was looking eagerly over his father's shoulder.

"Hi!" said Bert. "Wait till you hear Daddy's news!"

"We have news, too," said Flossie, excited. Quickly Nan told their adventure.

"Brave Lobo!" said Mrs. Bobbsey when the story was finished. She hugged the animal.

"You know what I think!" exclaimed Bert. "I'll bet Tommy Cheechoo caught these two men burying something in the clearing. They could have overpowered him and carried him away."

"I've been thinking the same thing," said Nan. "It would explain why his trail vanished there." She went on to tell the children's suspicions about the stolen gold and the illegal prospecting.

Her father looked thoughtful. "It's possible the men have a double game," he agreed.

"Whatever they were doing," said Bert, "I bet it's mixed up somehow with the four-winged blackbird."

"Little Moose," said Nan, "your father flies all over this territory. Did you ever hear him talk about such a bird?"

The boy shook his head. "No, but maybe my grandmother knows about it. You can come to see her this afternoon and ask."

"Good idea," said Bert. "I think we ought to go to that clearing, too, and find out what's buried there."

"Yes," said Mr. Bobbsey. "Meanwhile, I will

drive into Timmins and report Tommy's disappearance to the Ontario Provincial Police."

Mrs. Bobbsey asked Little Moose to stay for lunch and he accepted. Quickly the girls and their mother served sandwiches, milk, and cupcakes. Afterward Mr. Bobbsey left at once for town.

Little Moose thanked Mrs. Bobbsey for the meal. "You come with us, please," he said. "My grandmother will be glad to see you."

"Let's take her a present," said Nan.

"Why don't you make up a package of goodies from the things I bought in Timmins?" suggested Mrs. Bobbsey.

While Nan did this, the others quickly tidied the cabin. Soon they were hurrying along the path with the wolf following. Nan had the gift and her twin carried a trowel he had found in the shed.

On the way Little Moose told them that his grandmother was a Cree princess.

Flossie's eyes grew round and she said, "Does she wear a crown?"

Little Moose smiled. "You'll see. Her name is Princess Maggie Deer."

The little girl skipped happily. "I can't wait to meet her!"

"First we're going to do some digging in that clearing," said Bert.

But when they arrived, the children stopped

in dismay. Instead of three mounds of earth, they saw a trio of empty holes in the ground.

"Somebody beat us to it," exclaimed Freddie.

"The two men, I bet," said Nan.

"You probably scared them this morning," guessed her mother, "and they were afraid to leave the buried things here."

The children kicked the loose dirt around the edges of the holes and felt into them, but there was nothing to be found. Little Moose led the Bobbseys into a path on the left side of the clearing, and they went on through the woods. Soon they reached a dirt road.

"Is this the same one your father had his jeep parked on this morning?" asked Bert.

"Yes. It comes out onto the main road. We go the other way," the Indian added and started to follow the tire ruts.

In a little while they came to a small cabin. Little Moose went inside. He returned almost immediately and motioned the Bobbseys to enter.

They stepped into the main room. It was furnished with a table, several chairs, and an oil stove. There were three bunk beds, each covered with a colorful blanket. A tiny woman sat in one of the chairs.

Princess Maggie had a wrinkled face, long black hair, and little dark eyes which sparkled with humor.

"Are—are *you* Princess Maggie?" Flossie asked, her voice full of disappointment.

"Yes." The woman held out a hand to the little girl. "Some day, if you like, I tell about my dad, who was big Cree chief."

"I'd like to hear that," said Nan.

Little Moose introduced his friends, then reminded his grandmother about Tommy Cheechoo's message.

She replied rapidly in Cree. The boy turned to the Bobbseys. "My grandmother says she remembers now that her cousin has such a bird. Perhaps it is the one Tommy meant. I will take you there."

Nan then gave the old woman the gift. Her eyes sparkled at the sight of cookies and candy. She thanked the Bobbseys warmly.

Then her grandson led the twins up the road some distance to a scattering of shacks. Outside one of them sat a white-haired man in a buckskin jacket. Little Moose introduced the children to him and told them this was Brave Elk, Princess Maggie's cousin. The old man gave them a friendly, toothless smile.

"Brave Elk makes beadwork and sells it," said Little Moose, pointing to the colorfully beaded pillows and belts which lay on a wooden table beside him.

In Cree, Little Moose asked the artist about a four-winged blackbird. With a proud look the old Indian held up a pillow made of moosehide. On it was a crude design in beads.

"He says this is a four-winged blackbird," Little Moose told the Bobbseys.

The children's faces fell. "I don't see how this can be the one Tommy meant," Bert remarked. "Thank him for us, Little Moose, but I'm afraid it doesn't explain the warning."

As they were about to leave, the Indian boy picked up a wooden bear from a row of figures on the table. "Brave Elk also carves animals," he said. "He gave Tommy one of a moose, which he carries with him everywhere. Here's a large model of it."

The children examined the carving carefully. "It's very life-like," said Bert.

On the way back, Nan asked Little Moose what he did in the winter. The boy replied that he lived with his father in Moose Factory.

"That's an island in James Bay, north of here," he said. "Next fall I should go to high school," he added sadly, "but we have none there and I cannot afford to go away to one."

As the group went on through the woods, Nan looked thoughtful.

Back at Princess Maggie's the children reported that they had not found the four-winged blackbird. Flossie said solemnly, "I'm going to find it, though!"

Bert ruffled her curls affectionately.

"That's the wrong bird," Nan said

"I'm going to catch fish now," said Little Moose, bringing a pole from the cabin. "Come along, I'll show you Beaver Lake."

Bert and Freddie agreed at once. But the girls and Mrs. Bobbsey stayed with his grandmother.

"We want to hear about your daddy," Flossie pleaded.

Princess Maggie's English was halting but her little black eyes sparkled as she told the girls that her father had been called Man Who Gives The War Whoop.

"In those days," she said, "Cree tribe ruled all land up to Hudson Bay. We drove Sioux tribe west to great plains."

Then she went on to tell tales about going trapping with her father to get beaver skins, which they sold to the white traders.

The girls were begging for more stories when their brothers came back followed by the Indian with a long string of fish.

"How wonderful!" Mrs. Bobbsey exclaimed. "You must be a good fisherman, Little Moose!"

His grandmother smiled proudly. "He bring me fish all summer. You stay and eat with us?"

The family accepted and Little Moose dashed off to Cedar Camp to invite Mr. Bobbsey. By the time the two returned, a campfire crackled in front of the cabin and the smell of frying fish filled the air. Soon the meal was ready, with a share set out in a pan for Lobo.

After the first flaky bite of fish, Flossie said, "This is yummy!"

While they ate, the children told their father what they had done that afternoon. In turn, he reported that the provincial police had started searching for Tommy.

Long after the food was gone, the friends sat around the fire while the wolf dozed beside Nan. Darkness fell as they talked.

Suddenly Lobo gave a low growl and sat up.

"What's the matter?" asked Bert.

The animal bounded out of the firelight and disappeared among the trees. At the same time there came a startled cry from the woods.

"Run!" shouted a deep voice.

Bert leaped to his feet. "Come on!" he cried. "Let's catch those men!"

CHAPTER VIII

A SEAPLANE SEARCH

SWIFTLY Little Moose and Mr. Bobbsey left the campfire and followed Bert. For a few moments they stumbled along blindly, not used to the sudden darkness. "Wait," said Bert. "Listen."

The sound of crashing underbrush grew fainter as the prowlers ran away. A moment later the wolf suddenly appeared.

"Good old Lobo," said Mr. Bobbsey. "You chased the bad men away."

"But you did too good a job," Bert added, patting the wolf. "We wanted to catch them."

The trio returned to the campfire with Lobo and reported what had happened.

"Why do bad men spy on you?" asked Princess Maggie.

"We're not sure," replied Bert. "Maybe they know we're looking for Tommy and want to hear our plans."

"I bet it was one of them who searched our cabin," said Nan.

"Probably they wanted to find out who we were and why we had come to Cedar Camp," her twin remarked.

After a little more talk, the Bobbseys thanked Little Moose and his grandmother for a delicious supper, then said good night. When they reached their own cabin, Nan suddenly remembered the papers her parents and Bert had been studying.

"Daddy, you never told us your news," she said.

He smiled. "We've all been so busy, it skipped our minds. The papers you saw were a report on this land. There are evidences of valuable minerals here," he explained. "Mr. McLain advises a further survey."

"How 'citing!" Flossie exclaimed as Nan smiled happily.

"Will you have a gold mine, Daddy?" Freddie asked.

Mr. Bobbsey laughed. "I don't think so, but there are other important minerals in this area—copper, for instance. We'll have to wait and see."

"May I speak to you privately, Dad?" Nan asked.

"Certainly." Mr. Bobbsey and his daughter walked into the next room and conversed in low voices. They shook their heads when the others wanted to know what they were talking about.

"You'll find out some day," Nan said with a mysterious smile.

The next morning the Bobbseys drove into Timmins to the headquarters of the provincial police. Mr. Bobbsey introduced his family to Constable Leacock, the officer in charge.

"So these are the four detectives and their mother," he said, smiling. He was a broad-shouldered man with smooth dark hair. "Your dad has told me about you."

The twins blushed, but looked pleased. Then Bert and Nan reported all that had happened the day before.

"We think the two men are connected with Mr. Cheechoo's disappearance," said Bert.

The constable was impressed. "I'll give out their description and we'll see if they're living in town," he said. "More likely they're hiding out in some deserted lumber camp in the bush."

"And I bet that's where they're keeping poor Mr. Cheechoo," said Flossie.

"Yes," said the officer. "If anybody is living in the bush, we'll be able to see signs of it from the air. I'll get Jim Gordon to take up his plane and have Constable Thompson go along. Two pairs of eyes are better than one."

Quickly Nan gave her twin a meaningful look.

Bert grinned and spoke up. "Do you suppose my sister and I could go in the search plane, too, sir?" he asked eagerly.

The officer looked surprised, then said, "Good idea."

"How about Flossie and me?" asked Freddie.

Mrs. Bobbsey spoke up quickly. "No, dear. Not this time. We'll have fun some other way."

"May we go?" Bert turned to his mother and father.

"If you do exactly what the constable tells you," Mrs. Bobbsey said.

"Gordon's plane is based at Porcupine Lake," Constable Leacock told the twins. "You'll drive out with Bob Thompson now. He'll drop you at Cedar Camp on the way back."

Bert and Nan said good-by to the rest of the family and went with Constable Thompson, who was a husky young man with curly brown hair. A twenty-minute ride brought them to the shore of the lake.

"That's Gordon's plane." Bob Thompson pointed out a single-motored seaplane bobbing at the dock.

The twins were introduced to Jim Gordon, a lean, fair-haired young man. "Glad to have you aboard," he said cheerfully. "Hop in!"

Bert and Nan stepped onto the floats and up into the small plane. They took the two seats behind the policeman and the pilot. Gordon started the motor and they sped over the lake.

Nan peered from her window. "We're up!" she exclaimed as the water dropped below them.

The plane circled and turned north. It seemed to hang almost motionless in the air. Beneath them the children saw a vast expanse of trees dotted here and there by small lakes.

"See those paths down there?" Gordon shouted above the noise of the motor. When the twins nodded, the pilot told them the roads were made so the timber could be removed from the forest. "Tommy Cheechoo does that sort of work a lot," he explained. "I'll go as low as I dare. Keep a sharp lookout for smoke from a cabin or any signs of life, like discarded trash."

The little plane seemed to skim the treetops. The two men and the twins peered anxiously through the windows as they flew back and forth across the area.

Several times Nan pointed out small buildings below which were abandoned lumber camps. Each time, they sailed low over the cabins looking for smoke or litter but saw none. The searchers scanned the shores of the numerous lakes for evidence of a camp.

Suddenly the motor began to sputter. Gordon frowned as he made several adjustments. Finally he called to his passengers.

"I'll have to set down on one of the lakes. Fasten your seat belts!"

A few minutes later, the craft settled onto the calm waters of a small lake and taxied to shore. Then, stepping out onto the float, Gordon tied the plane to a nearby tree with a rope.

Constable Thompson, Bert, and Nan jumped to the narrow beach. "Will we have to stay here?" Nan asked anxiously.

Gordon smiled. "Until Bob and I get the engine fixed. It may take a while."

Bert looked at the lake curiously. "The water is clear brown now, but from the air it looked blue. Why is that?"

"When we were in the plane you saw the blue sky reflected in the water," said Thompson. "We call this a tea-water lake, because of the color. Seepage from the fir and spruce trees around it make it brown."

The twins walked to a log at the edge of the woods and sat down with their backs to the trees. They were quietly discussing the disappearance of Tommy when Nan suddenly stopped talking. She listened hard. *Was that a noise behind them?*

"I have a feeling somebody's watching us," she whispered.

Bert nodded. Slowly they turned around. Right behind them was a moose!

Nan screamed and jumped up as Bert bolted off the log. Instantly the big animal turned and fled into the woods.

"I have a feeling someone's watching us."

The children raced for the plane.

Both men were watching and laughing.

"You scared him more than he scared you," said Constable Thompson.

"Maybe," said Bert with a sheepish grin, "but I think it was a draw."

Meanwhile the young twins, their mother, and Lobo were walking up the path toward Princess Maggie's cabin. Flossie carried a big shallow baking pan with a napkin over it.

They found the Indian woman sitting by her door on a wooden chair. Little Moose was cleaning fish.

"We brought you a s'prise!" said Flossie, " 'cause you like sweets."

"We made it ourselves," said Freddie. "Mother helped."

The little girl handed Princess Maggie the pan. The old woman lifted the napkin.

"Fudge," said Flossie, beaming.

The princess smiled and patted Flossie's blonde curls. Then she passed candy around to everybody. After feeding a piece to Lobo, she ate one herself.

"Very good," she said. "Thank you."

"Super," said Little Moose with a grin.

Freddie pulled on the older boy's sleeve. "I have an idea," he said. "Those men last night must have left some tracks. Maybe we could follow them and find a clue to where Tommy is."

Little Moose agreed that it was a good idea. Mrs. Bobbsey gave permission, providing Lobo went and the twins stayed close to their Indian guide.

Taking the wolf, the children set off and followed the trail of crushed underbrush. It led to a shallow creek.

Freddie knelt on the bank. "Here's a big skid mark in the mud," he said. "Do you think the men went into the water?"

Little Moose nodded. "Yes." He examined the creek bed. "They walked upstream. You'd make a good Indian tracker, Freddie," he added and the little boy beamed.

"Let's wade," suggested Flossie.

Carrying shoes and socks, the three splashed along looking for signs of the two men while Lobo kept pace on the shore.

"Watch the rocks on the bank," instructed the guide. "If the moss has been scraped away, it was probably done by the men's boots. I don't think they stopped to remove them." He chuckled. "They were scared and ran into the water to throw the wolf off the scent."

A short time later, Flossie pointed to a boulder at the water's edge and cried out, "There!" White stone showed through gashes in the green moss.

"Yes, that's where the men left the creek," said Little Moose. "They went into the woods. See the broken brush on the bank?"

Quickly the children went ashore and put on their socks and shoes. The Indian boy followed the men's trail with the twins close behind and Lobo at their heels. Soon Freddie pointed through the trees to a huge gray stone. "That looks like the Devil Rock!"

"Yes. It's the back of it," replied Little Moose.

They came out into the clearing and gazed around, awed again by the strange idol.

"Look!" exclaimed Flossie. She ran to a small mound of fresh earth next to the big stone.

"Maybe those two men buried something here," said Freddie. "Let's see."

While Lobo watched, the three scooped the earth away with their hands. Freddie reached down and felt something lumpy. He pulled out a small leather bag.

"Gleeps, it's heavy," he said. He opened the drawstring and turned the sack upside down. Out poured a stream of grayish grains.

Flossie wrinkled her nose. "What's that?"

Little Moose's eyes sparkled. "It's gold ore!" he exclaimed.

CHAPTER IX

INTO THE PIT

SURPRISED, Flossie stared at the rocky grains. "It doesn't look like gold," she said.

"Why isn't it yellow?" asked her twin.

"This is the ore which contains the gold," the Indian boy replied. "It has to be processed in order to get the precious metal out."

Freddie looked excited. "Didn't I tell you those fellows were stealing from the mine?"

"But we can't be sure this is stolen gold," Little Moose said. "Maybe it belongs to the men."

"That could be," admitted Freddie. "I guess we'd better put it back."

Flossie glanced around uneasily at the woods and the ancient rock towering over them. "I wonder where the men are now?" she said. "It would be terrible if they came back and found us here."

As the twins quickly scooped the gold into the bag, Little Moose felt around in the loose earth at the bottom of the hole in the ground. "There's more here!" he exclaimed.

Swiftly the children dug deeper and found ten sacks of gold in all.

Suddenly Lobo's hair bristled and he growled softly. Little Moose seized his collar. After a minute the wolf relaxed.

"Hurry!" whispered Freddie. "Let's get out of here." Hastily the children reburied the gold.

Half an hour later they were pouring out the story to Mrs. Bobbsey and Princess Maggie.

"We must go and tell your father," said the twins' mother. "I think he's back by now."

The Bobbseys said good-by to Little Moose and his grandmother and hurried to Cedar Camp. They found Bert and Nan talking to Mr. Bobbsey on the porch.

"Did you find Mr. Cheechoo?" asked Flossie, running up to them.

"No," said Nan. "Not a sign of him."

While the older twins told of the seaplane adventure, Flossie and Freddie could hardly wait to tell their own story. After hearing it, Mr. Bobbsey drove to town at once to report the buried gold to the police. When he returned several hours later he told his family that the officers had gone to investigate.

Next morning Mr. Bobbsey announced that he had to see his lumber friend in Timmins. "Bert, I'd like you to return the mineral report to Mr. McLain," he added. "I'll drop you off and you can come home in a taxi."

Freddie asked to go along, and about mid-morning the two boys entered the main building at the mine. They went directly to the superintendent's office. Since Mr. McLain was busy, they left the papers with his secretary and returned to the hall.

"Let's wait a few minutes," Bert suggested. "Maybe a tour will end soon and we'll see our friend with the scar. I've got an idea about him."

Before long a group of tourists entered, followed by a crowd of miners.

Bert nudged Freddie. "There he is! He has a beard today. Keep an eye on him. I'll tell Mr. McLain!"

Bert ran into the superintendent's office. But the secretary refused to let him see the busy official. Finally she heeded Bert's pleas, and he told his news to Mr. McLain.

"Maybe the miner passes gold to the tourist and that's how it's smuggled out of here," said Bert.

"That could be!" exclaimed Mr. McLain.

"He's gone!" came Freddie's voice as he dashed through the open office door. Breathlessly he reported that the man had bumped into one of the miners, then hurried to the room where visitors leave their mine clothes. A few minutes later he had jumped into a waiting taxi at the gatehouse.

"I heard him tell the driver to go to the sand claim," Freddie said. "Is that like our sandbox at home?"

"Yes," said Mr. McLain with a smile, "but much bigger. It's a huge pit several miles from here. Sand is taken out of it and put into the mine to replace the ore. This prevents cave-ins."

"How can we get there?" Bert asked.

"You'll go with Mr. Cobb, my Security Chief. He'll need you to identify the fellow."

A few minutes later a big black car drove up to the door. Next to the young driver sat a husky man with dark crew-cut hair.

"I'm Mr. Cobb," he said to the boys as they climbed into the back seat. "This is our driver, Pete."

The car roared out of the grounds and soon was humming down the highway. Suddenly Freddie leaned forward, and pointed straight ahead.

"What's that?" he exclaimed. A line of huge iron buckets was crossing the road on a cable about twenty feet in the air!

Mr. Cobb explained, "Those buckets travel on a continuous cable between the mine and the sand claim. They are filled with sand out there, carried to the mine, dumped and brought back to the claim. That is the longest line of its kind in the world," he added proudly.

Some time later the driver turned into a field near a tall, weathered, frame building. "This is the sand claim," Pete announced.

Looking around, Bert and Freddie saw no sign of a taxi or a bearded man. A little distance away was another frame structure.

"What's in there?" asked Freddie.

Pete replied that the buckets came into that building. "They're filled automatically, and go right out again on the return trip."

As Pete stopped the car, Mr. Cobb jumped out and hurried inside. A minute later he came out.

"Fellow's not there," he reported, "and the men haven't noticed a taxi. Let's try the sand pit."

As the car bumped along over rugged ground, Bert looked around the barren claim. "What do you suppose the fellow wanted in this place?"

Mr. Cobb shrugged. "Hard to say."

"Maybe the man passes the gold on to somebody who works here," Freddie suggested.

Mr. Cobb shook his head. "No! Out of the question!" he said shortly. "I know all these men personally. They would never rob the mine."

Several minutes later they reached the spot where a huge power shovel was digging sand out of the hollow and dumping it into trucks. While the security officer questioned the drivers, the boys looked down into the pit.

Deciding that the shovel operator had the best view of the area, Bert went over and signaled to him. The man shut off the motor and beckoned to the boy. Bert climbed up into the cab and explained their mission.

"I haven't noticed strangers," the operator said, "but I've been pretty busy. Like to see how this thing works?" he added.

The boy nodded eagerly. The motor was turned on and the huge shovel swung out over the pit. The driver moved some levers and the shovel dropped. Like a yawning monster, it scooped sand into its jaws and swung upward to dump the load into a waiting truck.

Fascinated, Bert watched through the window of the cab. Again the shovel went down for sand.

Suddenly Bert gasped. "Stop! Stop!" he shouted.

His brother was sliding down the side of the pit directly into the path of the shovel! Shouts came from above and the next instant, the huge iron jaws swung aside. The little boy slid past and landed on the bottom of the hole.

Quickly he struggled to his feet and began to scramble up the slope. But for every step up, he slid back two.

"Stop! Stop!" Bert cried

"Bert! Help!" he cried.

"Take it easy!" bellowed Mr. Cobb. "We'll throw you a rope!"

Five minutes later the little boy was hauled to safety.

"You okay, Freddie?" asked his brother anxiously.

"Yes," was the reply. "I guess I got too close to the edge."

"You had us all scared," said Bert.

Red-faced, Freddie apologized, then thanked the men for rescuing him.

"We might as well go back," said Mr. Cobb. There's no sign of the man we're looking for."

It was noon by the time the boys reached Cedar Camp. Mr. Bobbsey had not yet returned, but the rest of the family heard the boys' story while eating lunch.

Afterward, Little Moose appeared and invited the twins to go fishing. Mrs. Bobbsey gave permission.

As the friends started off into the woods, Bert told the Indian about their morning's adventure. After half an hour's walk, Little Moose told the girls they were near Beaver Lake.

"What's that?" Freddie asked as they became aware of a clattering, whirring sound above them.

The children peered up into the sky. A helicopter passed slowly over the treetops.

"It looks like a great big blackbird!" Flossie cried.

"A blackbird!" Nan echoed. "Do you suppose—?"

"Some helicopters have four blades!" Bert exclaimed. "Could a 'copter be Tommy's four-winged blackbird?"

"But why would he warn Dad to 'beware' of a helicopter?" Nan looked bewildered.

"I don't know," Bert admitted. "But that one was real low, as if it were about to land. Let's see if we can locate it!"

"I found the four-winged blackbird!" Flossie trilled. "I found it!"

Bert ruffled Flossie's hair teasingly. "But we'd better hurry or it'll get away!"

The children trotted in the direction the helicopter had taken. For a few minutes they could hear the whirring of the rotor then there was silence.

"It has come down!" Little Moose broke into a run, with the twins close behind.

A short while later the searchers came to the edge of a clearing. "There it is!" Freddie cried.

The black and silver helicopter stood in the middle of the open space with no sign of life around it. The children went forward cautiously.

The steps leading to the small cabin were down. Bert started to climb them.

"Be careful!" Nan warned. "Someone may be inside!"

Very quietly her twin peered into the cabin. "There's no one here," he reported a moment later, and tried the door. "It's locked."

"That's funny," Freddie spoke up. "I wonder where the pilot went."

Little Moose pointed to the ground. "One set of footprints, heading toward the lake."

The next moment there came the sound of an airplane starting. The children looked at one another and began to run toward the gleam of water.

"There it is!" Flossie shouted.

Beside a small dock stood a seaplane. The door was open and two men were pushing a third man into the craft.

"Tommy!" Little Moose shouted. "That's Tommy Cheechoo!"

The two men looked around, startled. They gave the other one a final shove, then jumped in themselves. The door was slammed shut and the plane taxied out onto the lake!

"Oh!" Flossie cried out. "Those men are stealing Mr. Cheechoo!"

"One was the bearded man!" exclaimed Nan.

Bert looked grim. "And the other was the fellow with the scar!"

CHAPTER X

MOOSE FACTORY

"STOP! Stop!" yelled the children, running onto the dock. But, of course, the seaplane soared off the water and disappeared northward.

"Oh dear!" Flossie wailed. "Poor Mr. Cheechoo."

"We'll report it to the police," Bert assured her. "Perhaps they can find the plane."

Unhappily the twins and Little Moose turned away. "Anyway," said Bert, "now we know for sure the two men who buried the gold are part of the high-graders' gang."

"The red-faced man was piloting the plane," said Nan. "I saw him."

As they walked back into the woods Little Moose spotted the men's tracks, and a deep mark between them. "You can see they were dragging Tommy," he said.

The children followed the marks to a shack in the clearing.

"This must be where they held him prisoner," Bert said.

He and Nan stood on tiptoes and peered into the rear window, which was up high. The shack had only one room containing four cots, some chairs, a crude table, and an old iron cook stove. Across one wall was a shelf piled with rodlike objects.

Bert motioned Little Moose to look. "This is a core shack," the Indian boy declared when he saw the full shelf.

"What's that?" Freddie asked.

Little Moose explained that when prospectors wanted to find out if there were valuable minerals, they drilled down into the rock beneath the soil for samples, or cores. "Someone is using this place to store these."

"They're from Daddy's land, I'll bet," said Nan.

Bert tried the cabin door, but it was locked. "The police will have to search this and the helicopter," he said.

As they walked to the clearing, the children saw footprints showing that one man had gone from the 'copter to the shack.

"Where could they be taking Tommy?" Nan wondered.

"There are not many settlements north of here," the Indian replied, "except the ones on James Bay—like Moose Factory or Moosonee."

"Maybe they turned off in another direction," suggested Bert, "or are heading for a cabin in the bush."

"Can't we go to Moose Factory, anyway, and look for Mr. Cheechoo?" Flossie asked.

"We really ought to take the chance," agreed Nan.

"But how—" Bert began.

"I know!" Little Moose broke in. "My father has his plane on Trapper Lake, ready to fly to Moose Factory. He will take us along!"

"Say! That's a great idea!" Bert exclaimed. "We'll have to ask Mother and Dad, though."

The five children hurried back to Cedar Camp. Mr. Bobbsey had just come back from town. Listening to the story of Tommy Cheechoo, he looked grave.

"This is very serious," he said. "We must notify Constable Leacock. He'll handle it."

"But *we* want to save Tommy," Freddie burst out. "Little Moose's daddy will take us."

"But I can't leave here now," said Mr. Bobbsey.

"I'll go," said Mrs. Bobbsey. "This is a good chance for the twins to see the James Bay area."

"Oh, thank you, Mommy!" Flossie flung her arms around her mother.

While Mr. Bobbsey drove to town and reported the kidnapping to the police, Little Moose ran home to tell his grandmother where he was going. Meanwhile, the others packed.

When Mr. Bobbsey returned, the travelers said good-by to Lobo and left. With Little Moose pointing the way over the narrow dirt roads, the twins' father drove the party to Trapper Lake. There they found Big Moose just about to take off.

"Dad," Little Moose burst out, "will you fly us to Moose Factory? We think maybe Tommy Cheechoo is being taken there." Quickly Bert told the astonished Indian what had happened.

"I agree we must look for Tommy," Big Moose declared solemnly. "I was just about to fly some supplies up to the Lodge at Moosonee. If the little ones will sit on my cargo, I will be able to take you all."

The twins and their mother hugged and kissed Mr. Bobbsey, then got into the plane. With a roar, it soared off.

Dusk was falling when the pilot told his passengers to fasten their seat belts.

"That's Moose Factory," said his son, pointing to a large island in the wide mouth of the Moose River. The children could see rows of neat houses with bright-colored roofs, and a white church.

The next moment the plane came down on the water and taxied to the dock on the mainland.

"Hey, Big Moose!" called a man working on a boat.

"Dad, will you fly us?" Little Moose cried

"Hi, Ed!" the pilot responded, hopping out. "Has anyone flown in here today?"

"Yes," the man answered as the passengers jumped to the dock. "A seaplane came in about an hour ago with three fishermen."

"Where is it?" Bert asked eagerly.

"Oh, it was a rented job. Another customer took the plane back south."

"Was Tommy Cheechoo on it?" Big Moose asked.

"No. I never saw any of the men before. They're up at the Lodge if you want them."

"They can't be the ones we're looking for," Nan said in a discouraged tone.

"The men might have landed up the river, and come in by canoe," said Little Moose. "They could have come ashore without being seen."

"Ed, here, will take you all up to the Lodge along with the supplies," the pilot put in. "Little Moose and I will go home to Moose Factory. We'll start searching in the morning."

The Bobbseys piled into Ed's dilapidated truck which was parked nearby. A short drive brought them to a large white house on the street facing the river. A sign over the porch said, *Lodge*. The travelers were met outside by the pleasant-looking hostess.

"My name is Mrs. Michaels," she said, and led them to a row of small log houses behind the

Lodge. She took them into a cabin with green shutters.

The rooms were cozy with bright-colored curtains and bedspreads in Indian designs. Mrs. Bobbsey and the girls were settled in one and the boys in another across the hall. The doors of the other two rooms were closed.

After dinner in the main house and a walk around the town, they all went to bed. Bert and Freddie were just drifting off to sleep when the front door of the cabin opened. They heard the sound of heavy footsteps and deep voices.

"Maybe they're the three fishermen," Freddie thought. Sometime later he awoke to the sound of men talking. The voices seemed to be right in his ear! He sat up in bed and looked around. *Who was there?*

Then Freddie realized the speakers were in the next room. Their words could be heard easily through the chinks between the logs:

"Harry's coming Wednesday—on the Polar Bear!"

"That's a long time," a voice farther away replied.

"Well, we can always go fishing!" the first voice declared.

Nothing more was said. Freddie lay down, puzzled, and soon was dreaming of a man riding on a big white bear.

The following day was Sunday. After the

Bobbseys had been to church, Little Moose and his father appeared. "We came in our canoe," said the boy, "but we will search on foot."

All day the Bobbsey party explored Moosonee and the bush around it. There was no sign of the missing man or his captors.

"Tomorrow we will try at Moose Factory," the Big Indian promised, as they parted wearily.

The next morning right after breakfast Little Moose appeared and took them to the dock where Big Moose was waiting with a large canoe.

"What a giant!" Flossie remarked when she saw the wooden craft. It could seat at least ten people. There was an outboard motor at the back.

"We call them freight canoes," Little Moose explained. "They're built by the Indians over at Rupert House, a town on James Bay."

The twins and their mother stepped in and took seats. Little Moose stationed himself in the bow while his father steered from the stern.

"We'll start searching on Moose Factory," said the pilot.

As they sped across the wide river they passed a number of islands. They also saw several other canoes, which the Indians saluted.

"I guess the people here have canoes the way we have cars back home," Bert observed.

Little Moose nodded. "In these parts we go in

boats or planes. Not many automobiles."

Big Moose steered smoothly toward Moose Factory, and soon pulled up to a dock. His son jumped out and tied the canoe.

"Where are we going first?" Freddie asked as they all got out.

"To the end of the island where many of the Indians live," said Big Moose. "I will question them. They may have seen strangers around."

By this time the search party had climbed up the embankment to an old station wagon which stood in an empty lot. Everyone got in and Bert sat next to Big Moose. "Four gears!" he observed. "It must be a foreign make."

Big Moose grinned and nodded. "I fly planes but I do not often drive cars. I use only two gears. It is easier that way!" He started the motor, put the car into gear, and it lurched off.

He drove along a dirt road past houses and a school. Finally they came to a number of small dwellings, some made of wood, others of corrugated iron. Lines of bright-colored wash hung outside many of them. Big Moose parked the car and everyone got out. He started toward a stout Indian woman standing in a doorway. Chained nearby was a large gray furry dog.

"Oh look!" cried Flossie, "what a pretty doggie!" She ran eagerly toward the animal.

"Stop!" shouted Little Moose. "Flossie, stop!"

CHAPTER XI

THE A-OK SECRET

AT the Indian boy's warning cry, Flossie halted in her tracks. An instant later the dog sprang the length of his chain, snarling.

"Oh!" cried the little girl and scampered back.

"You mustn't touch the dogs!" warned Little Moose. He explained that most of those on the island were Huskies and not friendly. "That's why they're all chained," he added.

"You'd better stay close to the rest of us, Flossie," said her mother firmly.

While Big Moose conversed with the Indian woman in her own language, the Bobbseys listened. When he was finished, he told them that she had not seen the three strangers or Tommy Cheechoo. Big Moose thanked her, then spoke to other Indians, but none had seen the men.

The searchers drove around the island, stopping here and there to ask their question. Everywhere the answer was the same.

"I doubt if the thieves or Tommy are in Moose Factory," said Bert. The others agreed.

A few minutes later, Big Moose stopped the car on the bank of the river. He pointed to a white frame building with a steeple. "A very interesting old church. I think you'd enjoy seeing it."

While Big Moose waited in the car, his son showed the Bobbseys the inside. Proudly he pointed out the altar cloths made of soft moosehide and embroidered in beads.

"They're beautiful!" said Nan.

"We have something I think you never have seen before," Little Moose said mysteriously.

"What's that?" Bert asked.

"We have bored holes in the floors so the water can come in!" the boy replied and grinned at the visitors' surprised looks.

"Bored holes in the floor!" Freddie repeated. "Why would you do that?"

Flossie looked around, wide-eyed. "Where are they?"

"I'll show you." Little Moose pointed to the floor under the pews. There were little wooden pegs sticking up at regular intervals. He pulled out one of the pegs. It was a piece of bough about six inches long and tapered at the end.

Freddie and Flossie peered through the hole. There was nothing under it but the ground. Little Moose explained that when the ice in the river broke up in the Spring, it often caused floods which spread over the island.

"One year the water came up and the church floated away from its foundation," he said. "But now when the river rises we pull out these plugs."

"I get it," said Bert. "The water comes into the church but doesn't move it. That's neat!"

On the way out, the young twins and Little Moose were last. Freddie noticed a thick rope hanging through a hole in the ceiling of the vestibule. "What's that for?" he asked.

"Pulling it makes the bell in the tower ring." Little Moose replied.

"I want to do it!" Freddie stretched his hand up toward the dangling end.

"No! You mustn't!" Little Moose looked alarmed.

"What would happen?" Freddie asked, a mischievous gleam in his eyes.

"Everyone would come running to the church to see what was the matter!"

"Gleeps! That would be fun!" said the little boy. Reluctantly, he walked away from the bell rope and followed the others into the car.

"I will drive you now to Staff House," Big Moose declared. "Mrs. Martin will give you lunch."

On the way, the Indian explained that the Staff House was one of the oldest buildings on the island. It was maintained by the Hudson's Bay Company as a place for their employees to live. "Visitors use it as a hotel," he continued.

The station wagon stopped before a large white frame house and everyone got out. As Big Moose ushered the Bobbseys into the small hall a stout white-haired woman bustled up to them. The Indian introduced her as Mrs. Martin.

"I'm so glad you came," she said warmly.

Promising to be back after lunch, Big Moose and his son left. When the Bobbseys had washed their hands and faces, Mrs. Martin took them into the dining room.

A dozen men sat eating around a large table. They smiled and called cheerful greetings as the hostess seated the Bobbseys at the places which were set for them.

Passing bowls and platters, the other diners saw to it that the newcomers soon had heaping plates. The meal ended with giant slices of apple pie.

"Everything's big up here," said Freddie, "the woods and the river and even the pie."

A short time later, Little Moose and his father arrived. They invited the Bobbseys to have supper with them. The big Indian grinned. "I will have a surprise for you."

He drove off to attend to some business and Mrs. Martin invited Mrs. Bobbsey into a comfortable-looking living room for a visit. The twins arranged to meet her at the Indian's house later. The children went out for a walk. "Would you like to meet the Mountie who is stationed on the island?" Little Moose asked.

"Oh yes!" said Nan.

"What's the real name of the Mounties?" Freddie wanted to know.

"The Royal Canadian Mounted Police," Bert replied.

"Will this one be wearing his red coat?" Nan asked.

Little Moose grinned. "You'll see."

He led the Bobbseys toward a white house. In the front yard was a tall, handsome young man in khakis. Little Moose introduced him as Sergeant Bruce.

"Where's your red coat?" Freddie asked. He looked disappointed.

"It's hanging in my closet," the sergeant assured him. "I only wear it on parade." Then, noticing the twins' wistful expressions, he asked, "Would you like to see it?"

"Oh, please!" Nan replied.

Sergeant Bruce went into the house and came back a few minutes later wearing a bright red jacket, black breeches with a yellow stripe down the side, leather riding boots, and his wide-brimmed hat.

"You look bee-yoo-ti-ful!" Flossie cried.

"Can I dress up like a Mountie?" Freddie asked.

"Certainly," the man replied. "Here, try on this coat." He peeled off his tunic and helped Freddie into it. Then he put the wide hat on the boy's head.

The others rocked with laughter. The coat sleeves covered Freddie's hands and nearly reached the ground. And the hat almost covered his nose! Just the same, Freddie marched around proudly singing, "I'm a Mountie!"

When the fun was over, Freddie handed back the coat and hat.

The officer smiled. "You'll have to see a Mountie parade sometime. That is really a grand sight."

"Where is your horse?" asked Freddie.

The officer pointed to a jeep parked nearby. "On the island I use that. Nowadays we ride horses mostly for special occasions."

While all this had been going on, Bert had been thinking about Tommy Cheechoo. He told the Mountie about searching for the Indian.

Sergeant Bruce nodded. "The provincial police received a radio alert yesterday afternoon from Constable Leacock in Timmins. We've been watching for the seaplane, but only one came in. There were three fishermen on it. They did not answer the description of the wanted

"I'm a Mountie," Freddie sang

men, though. They were all wearing beards."

After thanking him for putting on his uniform, the children said good-by. The sergeant wished them luck in their search.

During the rest of the afternoon, Little Moose showed the twins some of the sights of the island. One was the powder house, a small stone building which had been used to store ammunition in the old days. Another was a museum with a blacksmith's shop in it. They also visited a sawmill and watched some Indian children run a sack race in the schoolyard.

Finally Freddie said, "I'm getting tired of seeing things. Could we rest?"

Little Moose laughed. "It's nearly suppertime. I'll take you to my house."

They walked down a street near the church to a small white frame building with a red roof. As they reached the front door, Big Moose drove up with Mrs. Bobbsey.

The two Indians were good cooks and before long everyone was sitting around the dining room table enjoying ham and corn with biscuits.

Suddenly Big Moose looked at his watch. Putting down his fork, he stood up.

"Come quick, everybody!"

Bewildered, the Bobbseys followed their hosts into the next room. On a table stood radio equipment. Big Moose adjusted several dials. "Now listen!"

"Hello, Bobbseys!" came a familiar voice.

"Daddy!" the children chorused and their mother beamed.

"I'm calling from the police radio room in Timmins," said Mr. Bobbsey. "Constable Leacock and Big Moose arranged for me to talk to you tonight. Are you all well?" he added.

The children chorused that they were and asked how he was.

"I'm fine—and so's Lobo. But we both miss you."

"We don't have any news of Tommy, Dad," said Bert. "Maybe they didn't bring him here."

"There's no lead at this end, either," said Mr. Bobbsey. "When the police went out to Devil Rock they found only an empty hole where the gold had been buried."

"I guess the men took it with them," said Bert, "or buried it somewhere else."

After they had all talked, Mr. Bobbsey suddenly said, "I almost forget! Nan, you know the secret you spoke to me about? Well, it's all fixed—A-OK!"

Nan's eyes sparkled. "Oh, Dad, thank you!" she exclaimed. "That's super!"

"I'm not sure yet when we'll be back, Dick," said Mrs. Bobbsey, "but don't worry about us."

Then everyone said good-by and their caller signed off.

"What a wonderful surprise," said the children's mother to Big Moose. "Thank you so much!"

"What's the A-OK secret?" asked Freddie.

"I can't tell you now," replied Nan. "You'll find out!"

The happy party went back and finished dinner. Afterward, the visitors helped wash the dishes and clean up the kitchen.

"Now we'd better be going," said Mrs. Bobbsey. "It's dark already." Big Moose said he would take them back to Moosonee right away.

Little Moose picked up a flashlight from a table and opened the front door. As Bert stepped out first, a dark figure wearing a stocking mask darted across the porch and vaulted over the railing.

"Stop!" cried Bert and leaped over after him. Grabbing wildly, the boy caught the fleeing man's shirt front. But the fellow tore free, leaving a scrap of cloth and something hard in Bert's hand.

"After him!" cried Big Moose as he and the boys chased the prowler, but the man had melted into the darkness.

Back on the porch, Bert put out his hand and said, "Turn on your light, Little Moose."

The Indian boy aimed the beam onto Bert's palm. Beside a scrap of red cloth lay a large shining lump.

"The fool's gold!" Nan exclaimed.

CHAPTER XII

A BUSH FIRE

"THE bad man must be on the island!" exclaimed Flossie, staring at the shining ornament in Bert's hand.

"Yes," said her older brother excitedly, "this is the ball of pyrite that fellow was wearing!"

"He was spying on us," said Freddie.

"Oh, if only we could catch him," said Nan, "we'd probably be able to find the other two men and Tommy Cheechoo!"

Big Moose shook his head. "My guess is the spy will get off the island as fast as he can. He'd be gone before we could find him."

Suddenly an idea hit Freddie. "Not if everyone on the island searches!" he said. "The Mountie could ask them to do it."

"That would take too long," said Bert. "By the time you go to Sergeant Bruce and—"

"No, no!" insisted Freddie, hopping in excitement. "I know a way! Come on!"

He dashed off the porch and raced down the road toward the old church.

"Where are you going?" his mother cried.

"To call everybody! Come on! Hurry!" Minutes later he dashed into the church. "Now's my chance to ring the bell!" he told himself. "That will bring all the people here!"

The end of the rope dangled just out of the little boy's reach, but he jumped up and caught it. As the weight of his body pulled it down, the bell in the steeple gave a great *clang.*

"This is keen!" Freddie thought.

Then the bell swung the other way and the rope carried Freddie up into the air. "Whee!" he cried happily just as his family and friends dashed into the little hallway.

"Freddie!" Bert yelled above the sound of the bell. "Stop! That's enough!" He caught his brother and lifted him down.

"It's a wonderful idea, Freddie!" said Big Moose. As the others praised him, too, the little boy flushed with pride.

Hearing voices, they went outside again and saw people hurrying to the church from all directions. Sergeant Bruce ran up, and Big Moose quickly explained the emergency. Bert gave the officer the ball of pyrite.

When the crowd had gathered the sergeant briefed them and said, "Cover every inch of this island. Bring any strangers to me!"

"Whee!"

All the people nodded and hurried off. Soon many bicycle lamps, as well as a few car lights, could be seen going along the roads. Flashlight beams bobbed around houses and bushes and across the lots.

The Bobbseys hurried to the waterfront with their Indian friends and got into the canoe. Around the island they went looking and listening for a fugitive in a boat.

"We could easily miss him," said Bert, "since we can't be everywhere at once."

Finally they docked and went to the Mountie's house. "Has anyone found the man?" Bert asked.

"No luck," said Sergeant Bruce. "It was a fine idea, young man," he said to Freddie, "but the fellow probably sneaked out in a canoe. I'm inclined to think the men are in the bush on the mainland," he added. "It's easier to hide there."

"I'm worried about Mr. Cheechoo," Nan confessed.

"We all are," the officer replied. "Tommy has many friends here." He frowned. "From what you've told me, I'd say these men are daring and dangerous."

"They are plenty rough," Big Moose agreed. He turned to the twins. "Somehow they've found out you're here. From now on you must be especially careful."

The children promised. Then Bert said, "We

know the men came North in a seaplane. It must be hidden somewhere in this area. And also they have a canoe. If we could find either of those it might help us locate the hideout."

"Right," said the Mountie. "We'll send out scouting parties tomorrow and alert all bush pilots to look for the kidnappers and Tommy. The provincial police have a base at Moosonee," he explained, "and we will work together on it."

"I'd like you children to go in my plane tomorrow to help search," said Big Moose, "—if your mother permits."

Seeing the twins' eager looks, Mrs. Bobbsey agreed. The children thanked her and then Flossie yawned. "But we'd better go back to Moosonee now," their mother added. "I think we've had enough excitement for one night."

Early next morning the twins were ready and waiting on the dock. Flossie was still munching on an orange muffin she had taken from the breakfast table when the silver craft landed.

Little Moose opened the door. "Ready to work?" he asked with a grin as the children climbed into the cabin.

"Gee, we're getting used to having a seaplane at our disposal," Bert said jokingly as the pilot once again guided the plane into the air.

The Indian looked serious. "We'd better have sharp eyes today. After last night, the kidnappers probably know the search is on. They may clear out of this area soon—if they're not gone already."

"That would be awful," said Nan. "We might never find them."

As the plane flew along the mainland coast, Bert remarked, "It must be keen to be a pilot."

"My father's also a flying fire warden," said Little Moose proudly. He explained that when a bush pilot was licensed he had to agree to watch for forest fires and report them on his radio.

Freddie looked down at the close-growing trees. "How do they ever get fire engines in there?" he asked.

"They don't," said Little Moose. "When the blaze is deep in the bush, we just have to let it burn. But when the fire gets close to timber stands or settlements, we go in on the roads to fight it. Of course," he added, "we don't have the most modern equipment."

Noses glued to the windows, the children watched the wilderness below for signs of life. Suddenly Flossie gave a cry.

"Fire! Fire!" The little girl pointed excitedly out her window. "See, down there! Lots of smoke!" The children all looked out her side of the plane.

"Fasten your seat belts," ordered Big Moose. "It may be a brush fire, but we will investigate before calling the alarm."

"Oh boy!" exclaimed Freddie. "I wish I had

my little fire engine!" Playing fireman was his favorite game.

As soon as the plane had landed and taxied to shore, Little Moose tied it to a tree. The next moment, Freddie was out and running toward the billowing smoke that could be seen among the trees. The others quickly followed. The odor of charred wood was strong.

Abruptly the woods came to an end and the group found themselves on the edge of a clearing. Two men could be seen across the blackened field watching the fire burning ahead of them.

"They might have Tommy!" Flossie whispered.

"Maybe they're fireflys," Freddie surmised.

"Firebugs, Freddie," Bert corrected.

As they heard the group approaching, the men turned around and called greetings to Big Moose. One had a thin face, the other was square-jawed. Each had a rake in his hand.

"We're clearing this land so we can build our fishing camp," the thin man said as the searchers walked up to them.

"We saw the smoke from the air and decided we had better have a look-see," the Indian replied. "I didn't know you were planning to build here, Tom."

"We are," said the thin man. "But clearing this land sure is a job."

Big Moose introduced the children and explained about searching for Tommy Cheechoo.

"You haven't seen any strangers or a seaplane around here, have you?" asked Bert.

A strange look came over the faces of the two men. They glanced at each other.

"No plane," replied Tom, "but we saw three fellows with a canoe yesterday just before dawn."

"We'd gone down to the riverbank to fish for our breakfast," Bill explained. "Nearby, there's the mouth of a creek. It's pretty well hidden by heavy brush. All of a sudden we heard the putt-putt of a motor and a minute later out into the river came a canoe!"

The other man spoke up. "We called to the men and they hollered back—said they were campers."

"What did they look like?" Nan asked eagerly. "Couldn't say," replied Bill. "It wasn't really light yet, but we could see that two were big fellows. The other was a little shrimp. They had a large blanket roll propped up in the bow."

"And here's the odd part," put in Tom quickly. "I was sure I saw that roll moving!"

"I told Tom his eyes were playing tricks," said Bill, "but now I'm not so sure."

The twins looked excited. "I'll bet it was Tommy Cheechoo in the blanket," said Nan. "Which way were they going, Tom?"

"North—toward the river mouth."

"I bet Tommy was hidden near here," said Bert, "and when you started to clear the land, it scared the men out."

Bert spoke up quickly. "The place must be very close then. Let's try to find it. Maybe they left a clue."

"Good idea," said Big Moose.

"The creek is straight that way," said Tom, pointing the direction.

After thanking the two men, the search party headed into the woods again. Before long they reached a quiet stream.

"Which way shall we go?" asked Freddie.

"Let's split up," suggested Bert. "We can cover more ground in less time that way."

"Fine," said Big Moose. "I'll go downstream. The rest of you go up. We'll meet here." He stuck a broken branch upright in the muddy bank to mark the place and strode off.

Single file the children made their way along the creek, looking for signs of a camp. Soon, through the trees Bert spotted a small shabby tent.

"There it is!" he exclaimed. Quietly the searchers moved toward the camp. When they reached the little open space, they paused behind the trees and looked out cautiously.

Suddenly Flossie gave a frightened squeak and pointed to the tent. The sides had moved!

"Something is in there," Nan whispered.

CHAPTER XIII

THE WOODEN SEAHORSE

THE children watched one side of the tent shake, then the other.

"Maybe the bad men are in there," whispered Flossie, taking Nan's hand.

Bert walked quietly over to the shelter, followed by Little Moose. With a sudden movement Bert seized a canvas flap and threw it back.

Nothing happened.

The boys peered into the tent as the girls hurried over. Something was flapping about inside.

"A bird!" exclaimed Nan. Blindly the gray feathery creature hit the canvas, then flew across and bumped the other side.

"Poor thing," said Nan. "It's scared. Let's help it get out."

While the boys held both flaps open, the girls went in and shooed the bird toward the opening. It swooped out and flew away!

"That was a Canada jay," said Little Moose.

"How did it ever get in there?" said Freddie.

"I guess the campers left the tent open," said Bert, "and the jay flew in. The wind probably blew the flaps closed and the bird was trapped."

"Yes, that must be what happened," said Nan. "There are some cracker crumbs in a box in the tent. The bird probably went in for those."

The girls stepped into the little tent and looked around curiously. It was empty except for an old bare cot and the cracker box. "This can't be the kidnapper's camp," Nan remarked. "There's room for only one person in here."

While she spoke, Flossie had been looking at the cot. "There's some funny scratches on this wood," she said, running her finger over the leg of the bed.

Nan stooped to see them. "Maybe they mean something," she said.

"Let us see," said Bert. His sisters moved outside, giving the boys room to examine the marks.

"This is a message in the Cree language!" said Little Moose. "It says 'Help prisoner'."

"Tommy must have written it!" exclaimed Bert.

"This is the right place then!" said Freddie excitedly.

"What else does it say?" asked Nan.

"Nothing," replied the Indian. "I guess that's all Tommy had time for."

Carefully the children scoured the tent and

surrounding ground, but found nothing to tell them where Tommy Cheechoo's captors had taken him.

As they started back to meet Big Moose, Nan looked puzzled. "I don't understand," she said. "If Tommy was kept here, where did the men live?"

"There wasn't even a campfire," Freddie added.

"They must have camped someplace else," said Bert. "They wouldn't want anyone to see Tommy with them."

When the group reached the stick marker, they waited and soon Big Moose appeared. After the children reported what they had found, the party returned to the silver craft.

"There must be a cove or inlet around here," Bert said, "where the kidnappers hid their plane."

"We'll search from the air," said Big Moose.

For quite a while they flew along the coast, looking for the missing craft, but did not find it.

Suddenly Big Moose's radio began to squawk. The twins could make out only the words *doctor* and *hurry.*

"It's a mercy call," said the pilot. "There's a sick lady in Moose Factory who needs a special doctor. I have to fly her to Timmins right away!"

As Big Moose headed for the mainland dock,

his son explained that bush pilots often had to answer calls for help. "The other search planes will keep looking for Tommy."

Meanwhile Big Moose radioed a report to the police on what the Bobbsey party had learned and seen that morning. Then the Indian said to his son, "I want you to go with me on the mercy call. You can see how Grandma is getting along, while I do some errands in Timmins." A few minutes later he landed and let the Bobbseys out on the dock.

"We'll see you tomorrow," Little Moose called and the plane flew off across the river.

The children walked up to the lodge, arriving just in time to freshen up for lunch.

The girls put on fresh yellow pedal pushers, shirts, and sweaters. Then Flossie tied a white bandanna around her neck and Nan chose a blue one. Meanwhile the boys had changed to clean blue jeans and T-shirts.

Then they ate with their mother. She listened with interest to their adventures. "What will you do this afternoon?" she asked.

"I think we should go exploring around Moosonee," said Nan. "Who can tell—maybe we'll pick up a clue to where Tommy is."

"Good idea," her mother said.

Wondering what luck the other search planes were having, the twins strolled down to the riverbank. Bert and Freddie were trying to skip

stones across the rippling surface of the water
when an Indian boy of about twelve ran up to
them. He was wearing a blue sweater with a
design of white maple leaves on it.

"You come with me," he said, indicating a
large canoe drawn up on the bank a short distance away. "I show you man."

"What do you mean?" Bert asked. "What
man?"

The boy took hold of Bert's arm and tried to
pull him toward the canoe. "You come," he insisted.

"What man do you suppose he means?" Nan
asked.

"Maybe the one we chased last night!" Bert
remarked.

"Or maybe he knows where Mr. Cheechoo
is," Flossie said. "Let's go with him!"

"I'll run and tell Mother we're going," Nan
suggested.

"No! No time! Hurry!" The boy in the blue
sweater started toward the canoe.

Bert spied another Indian lad who had been
standing on the bank listening to the conversation. He hurried over to him.

"Do you speak English?" Bert asked. The boy
nodded. Bert pointed toward the lodge and
asked the boy to find Mrs. Bobbsey. "Tell her
we're following a clue," he said, "and we'll be
back soon."

The boy ran down the road and the twins got into the craft. Their guide started the motor and headed upstream. After about twenty minutes, they passed an island where Bert spotted the tip of a canoe sticking out of the underbrush.

Another island lay just beyond. The Indian boy ran the craft onto the beach of the second one and the twins jumped ashore. "Where is this man?" Bert asked.

"Come." The boy led the way into a wilderness of low trees and bushes.

The Bobbseys found it hard going. The undergrowth was thick and the brambles scratched the children's legs. Several times Flossie caught her foot in the long grass and fell.

"Take my hand, Floss," Bert said. They continued inland until the Indian boy suddenly stopped. He pointed ahead to a clump of trees and said, "Man!"

Freddie began to run toward the spot, followed by the others. They pushed forward eagerly among the trees, expecting any second to see the mysterious man. But there was no sign of him.

All at once Bert realized their guide was not with them. He looked back. The Indian lad was running toward shore!

"Hey!" Bert called out indignantly. "What's the big idea?"

"Catch him!" Flossie shouted.

"Oh!" Nan cried. "Maybe he's going to leave us on this island!"

Bert raced in pursuit, but the Indian had a head start. By the time Bert reached the beach, the boy was speeding off in the canoe.

"Stop!" Bert yelled.

The Indian paid no attention and swung the craft out into midstream. The dismayed twins watched as it sped away.

"Why do you suppose he did this to us?" Nan asked. "I never saw him before, did you?"

Bert shook his head. "It beats me!"

"Gleeps!" Freddie exclaimed. "We're ship-wrecked!"

"Maybe he's only teasing and will come back in a minute," Flossie suggested hopefully.

The twins sat down on a big log to wait. A half hour went by and the boy had not returned.

"I guess he isn't coming back," Bert declared finally.

"But what will we do?" Flossie was near tears.

Suddenly Bert had an idea. "I'll tell you what! Let's go over to the next island. There must be somebody there, because I saw a canoe!"

Freddie stared at his brother. "The next island!" he echoed. "How'll we get there?"

Bert grinned and patted the log. "We'll ride on this!"

Freddie grinned. "That's a great idea!"

"It isn't far," said Bert jumping up. "See, you could almost throw a stone from here."

Excited, the children began to drag the long log down to the water's edge.

"What if it tips over?" asked Flossie.

"We can all swim," said Nan. "Anyhow, we'll be careful. We'd better carry our sneakers," she added, and took them off. Peeling off her socks, she stuffed them into the shoes. "Tie the laces together," Nan instructed, "and hang them around your neck." The others followed her example.

Then Bert pushed the log into the water and held it steady. "Now everybody get on and sit astride," he ordered.

"It's like a wooden horse," said Flossie with a nervous giggle.

"A wooden *sea*horse," added Nan, taking her place in front.

When they were settled, Bert gave the log a shove outward, splashed through the shallows and climbed on the back. "Now everybody paddle!" he said.

The children leaned down and paddled with their hands. Slowly the strange craft went forward and finally bumped the opposite shore. Moments later the Bobbseys were all on the bank, red-faced and laughing.

"This way," said Bert and led off toward the side of the island where he had spotted the

"Now everybody paddle!" Bert ordered

canoe. In some places they had to climb over fallen tree trunks and jump inlets, but soon they reached a small cove.

"There it is," said Bert. They could see the tip of the craft peeping out from under overhanging bushes. They hurried to it and Bert pushed the branches aside. He gasped at what he saw.

"It's a wreck!" exclaimed Nan.

Broken fragments of wood were scattered about. Only the bow of the canoe was intact.

Bert looked disgusted. "This has been here for years," he said, kicking the mossy pieces of wood.

As they gazed around, Nan said suddenly, "Wait a minute! Someone has been here!" She pointed to a muddy patch on the bank a short distance away. "Footprints!"

Bert examined the tracks. "Several men have been here and more than once," he said. "See how the brush is trodden down." He peered into the woods. "They've broken a path."

"Let's follow it," suggested Nan.

With Bert in the lead, the twins made their way along the rough trail. Suddenly Nan stooped and picked up something.

Her voice trembled with excitement as she said, "Look what I found." In her hand lay a small carved moose!

"That's Tommy Cheechoo's!" exclaimed Bert.

CHAPTER XIV

A TREE HOUSE DISCOVERY

FOR a moment the twins could not believe their eyes!

"It looks just like Tommy's lucky piece," said Nan, examining the tiny carved moose.

Bert took the wooden animal from her and looked it over carefully. "This is exactly like the big model we saw at Brave Elk's," he said. "There couldn't be two like it."

"Hurry," said Flossie, "let's look for Mr. Cheechoo."

"We will," said Bert, "but go quietly. The thieves may be here, too."

"That's right," Flossie whispered. "I forgot."

The children followed the rough trail until it disappeared among the trees in the middle of the island.

"Now what?" asked Freddie.

"Keep looking," said his brother grimly.

They moved on, but saw no signs of human

life. Finally they reached the opposite shore and sat down, exhausted, on a narrow beach.

"We mustn't give up," said Nan. "I feel sure Tommy is on this island."

"But where?" Flossie asked, shaking the pine needles out of her moccasins.

"There is nothing here but trees, trees, trees!" Freddie said in a sing-song voice.

"Maybe he's in a treehouse," Flossie suggested.

"Oh, pooh," said Freddie. "People up here don't build treehouses. Especially on deserted islands."

"Why not?" Bert exclaimed, springing to his feet. The others looked at him in amazement. "Tommy has to be hidden somewhere and what would be better on an island like this than a treehouse?"

"Wow!" Freddie turned a somersault in his excitement.

"Oh, Bert, we've never thought to look in the trees when we were searching," Nan said. "We were always watching the ground for footprints or looking for a camp or a cabin."

Flossie jumped up. "Let's try to find the treehouse!"

"Everyone agreed?" Bert questioned.

"Yes," came the chorus of voices.

"Okay, let's go," said Bert.

Again the searchers started into the woods.

Progress was slow as they walked along, looking upward into the thick branches of fir, spruce, and tamarack.

"Ow!" cried Flossie as she stumbled, hitting her toe on a stone.

"Watch where you're going," said Nan.

"How can I look up and down at the same time?" grumbled Flossie.

Necks aching, the twins plodded on. After what seemed like a long time, Bert stopped abruptly. "Listen!"

The others paused. From somewhere was coming a dull thumping noise. Then the sound stopped.

"It was up ahead," said Bert softly. He put his finger to his lips and beckoned.

Warily the children moved on, then stopped to listen. The sound came again, loudly!

"It seems to be coming from above," whispered Nan. Tensely the children gazed into the treetops. Together they peered up into a big tamarack tree. And at the same time they spotted a crude wooden structure among the branches.

"A treehouse!" Flossie exclaimed.

THUMP!

"Tommy Cheechoo!" Bert called.

THUMP! THUMP!

"We've got to get up there!" said Bert, circling the tree. On the other side he saw huge nails which had been hammered into the trunk for footholds. As the girls watched anxiously, he climbed up. Freddie was right behind him.

On a platform among the limbs was a low-roofed house with a wooden door secured by a padlock.

Bert took out his pocketknife and managed to pry off one of the hasps. Opening the door, he peered into the box-like room. A man was sitting in a corner with his hands and feet bound!

"Mr. Cheechoo!" said Bert.

The man gave a hoarse croak. The boys realized that he was too weak to call, but had hit his heels on the floor for a distress signal.

Quickly Bert cut the prisoner's bonds. "Can you walk?" Bert asked anxiously.

The man moved his legs cautiously and groaned. "I try," he whispered.

The boys helped him to the edge of the platform. Then Freddie went down the trunk first, guiding Tommy's feet to the nails. Finally the man reached the ground.

The twins saw he was of medium height with coarse black, shoulder-length hair. He wore a faded blue shirt and trousers. Although his body was muscular, he looked thin and drawn. He leaned against the tree.

"We must get him to the beach," said Nan. "Maybe we can hail a boat from there."

The children helped Tommy Cheechoo along. His legs were stiff, but after a little

"Mr. Cheechoo!" Bert cried out

while he began to be able to walk more easily.

As they slowly made their way through the woods, the Bobbseys told the man how they had searched for him. In halting English he thanked them.

Reaching the beach, Nan explained how they came to be stranded. The rescued Indian did not seem particularly disturbed, he was so glad to be free. But he did warn the twins that his captors came every day, in mid-morning, to bring him food.

"I hope we'll be away from here by then," said Bert.

"I'm hungry," said Freddie.

"I guess we all are," remarked Nan.

"I have two chocolate bars I bought at the lodge," said Bert. As he took them from his pocket, he grinned. "They're kind of mashed."

"Come on, Floss," said Nan. "Let's pick berries."

The sisters went over to some bushes nearby and gathered blueberries which they put in Flossie's bandanna. When the scarf was full, the girls brought the fruit back to the others. Carefully Nan divided the berries and candy five ways. The twins and Tommy ate hungrily.

"It wasn't a big supper," said Flossie, "but it was good."

"Do you feel up to talking?" Bert asked the Indian.

Tommy nodded and in broken English, unfolded his story. The day the Bobbseys had been scheduled to arrive at Cedar Camp, he had taken a short cut through the woods to Princess Maggie's cabin. He had not gone far when he heard a roaring noise overhead, the same strange noise he had heard so many times before.

"The four-winged blackbird!" Flossie interrupted. Tommy nodded smilingly, and continued to talk.

This time he had decided to hide and watch. Maybe he could find out what the men in the blackbird were doing. The creature had landed in an open space near the lake and two men climbed out. They had several small, heavy bags which they carried to another clearing.

"By the path to Cedar Camp?" asked Nan.

The Indian nodded. He had watched from behind the trees, while the men dug three holes and buried the bags.

"I make no noise," he said. "Then—I go *achoo!*"

"You sneezed!" exclaimed Flossie. "And they heard you!"

"Men catch me and hit on head," said Tommy. "I wake in core shack—all tied up."

"Did you know they were stealing gold from the mine?" Freddie asked eagerly.

"Yes. They talk—I hear."

The Indian went on to say that the men flew

north because the Bobbseys and the police were searching for them.

"Put me in tent in bush," he continued. "No make fire for cook. Afraid somebody see. Bring cold food. Not much to eat."

"We found the message you scratched on the cot," said Flossie. "Little Moose read it for us."

The Indian looked surprised. With gestures and his small supply of words, he told them that the bearded man had dropped one of the big nails he used later to make the tree ladder. Though the prisoner's hands had been tied, he managed to lean over the cot edge, reach the nail and scratch the words in Cree.

"I guess you didn't really expect anybody to find them, way back in the bush, did you?" asked Nan.

The Indian shook his head. "No hope—but I try."

"Poor Mr. Cheechoo," said Flossie kindly. "You were very brave."

The man's dark eyes sparkled and he smiled.

"Yesterday the men brought you here in a canoe, didn't they?" asked Bert. As the Indian nodded, the boy remembered the carved moose. He took it from his pocket.

"Did you drop this on purpose?" he asked.

The Indian's eyes widened. "Where you find moose?"

Bert explained and the Indian shook his head.

"Men carry me on island. Very rough. Blanket fall off."

"I see," said Bert. "It must have dropped out of your pocket then."

The man nodded and took the little carving in his hand. Lovingly he rubbed the smooth wood.

"It really was your lucky moose," said Freddie, " 'cause it told us you were on this island."

Bert spoke up. "Where are the three men camping, Mr. Cheechoo?"

The Indian shrugged.

"Do you know where their plane is hidden?" Nan put in.

"No. They mad at you," added the Indian, shaking his head warningly. "No let men catch you."

"That reminds me," said Bert, "we've got to get away from here."

"I haven't seen a single boat all the time we've been talking," said Nan.

Bert glanced up at the evening sky. Black storm clouds were beginning to appear. "We'd better gather some wood," he said. "When it gets dark, we'll light a fire."

"A signal fire!" Freddie exclaimed in delight. He began to pick up pieces of driftwood from the ground. Soon the twins were all scurrying around, adding wood to a rapidly growing pile on the beach. Tommy Cheechoo had recovered enough to help.

"That will make a big blaze," Nan declared. "Someone is sure to see it and come for us."

Soon Bert judged it dark enough to light the fire. "Lucky thing I took this box of matches from the cabin," he remarked. "I was going to keep it for a souvenir."

A little wind had sprung up and blew out the match as Bert struck it. He used up half the box to get the fire started. When finally it caught and flared up, the twins heaved sighs of relief.

Then Flossie cried out. "I felt a raindrop!" A minute later rain came down in sheets. The fire flickered, hissed, and died out!

CHAPTER XV

SOS

"OH!" Flossie wailed. "It's awful dark! What will we do?"

"Get out of the rain first," Bert said practically.

The children and Tommy ran back into the shelter of the taller trees and crouched there until the cloudburst was over. Then they went back to the pile of wood.

"I'm sure it won't burn now," Nan said anxiously.

"Maybe there's dry wood underneath," replied Bert. The older twins lifted off the dripping pieces on top.

Tommy Cheechoo crouched down and felt the sticks beneath. He shook his head doubtfully. "I think no burn."

"Maybe if we had something really dry for kindling," said Bert.

The castaways looked around but found nothing usable.

"I know!" said Nan. "How about our handkerchiefs? They're dry 'cause they've been in our pockets."

"Good idea," said Bert. "Let's have them all."

Each of the twins gave him a clean white handkerchief and Tommy handed over a faded blue one, neatly folded. Bert stuffed the dry cloth carefully under the wood at the bottom of the pile.

"Now it'll burn, I bet," said Flossie hopefully.

"I'll find out." Bert struck a match and held it to the small sticks at the bottom of the pile. A wisp of smoke arose, but quickly died out. He tried several more times with the same result.

"There are only a few matches left," Bert said. "Do you have any, Mr. Cheechoo?"

"Name Tommy," said the Indian with a smile. Then he pointed to his pockets. "All gone."

"Then we'd better wait until morning," Bert decided. "The wood might be dry enough to catch by then."

"Do you mean we have to stay here all night?" Flossie's lower lip began to tremble.

"I'm awfully hungry," said her twin. "I sure wish we had something to eat!"

"Oh, Freddie, you can't be hungry," said

Nan. "You ate a huge pile of pancakes for breakfast and had a big lunch. Besides, you just finished a snack."

The boy sighed and plopped down on the beach.

"A boat! A boat! I see a boat," Bert cried out in excitement. Skimming down the river was a bright light! Across the water came the putt-putt of the motor.

The children jumped to their feet, waving and yelling as loudly as they could. But the craft passed the islands and disappeared.

"Oh dear." Flossie sadly returned to her perch on a rock.

Freddie slapped at his leg, then his arm. "The 'squitoes are terrible!" he said.

In an effort to cheer up the young twins, Nan suggested that they have a blueberry contest.

"How do you mean?" asked Freddie.

"You and Flossie will pick blueberries and whoever gathers the most wins."

"Is there a prize?" asked Flossie.

"Sure," said her sister. "There'll be a surprise for the winner when we get back to Moosonee."

"Who'll give it to us?" asked Freddie.

"I will," said Nan. She took the bandanna from her neck and tied two corners to Freddie's belt. "If you hold up the ends, it'll make sort of a bag." she instructed. Then she fixed Flossie's scarf in the same way.

"Come on," she said and led the young twins toward the bushes near the water where they had been picking earlier.

"Now work fast," she told them, "because when I say stop, you can't gather any more." She paused a moment. "Go!"

The children picked as quickly as they could in the dark, dropping the fruit by handfuls into the bandannas.

Freddie worked along the water's edge. Soon his way was blocked by a tree. Its tangled roots struck out into the river.

On the other side of the tree Freddie made out a thick clump of bushes, overhanging the water. Trying to reach it, he stepped out on the slippery roots. The next moment his foot slid between the two of them and stuck tight!

"Help!" he shouted. The other twins and Tommy ran to him.

"Stand still, Freddie!" Bert said. "I'll get you out."

With the Indian holding him by the belt, Bert leaned over, grabbed Freddie under the arms and gave a heave. The boy's foot came free and his brother helped him ashore.

"Thanks, Bert!" Freddie exclaimed. "I was sure I was going in the river!"

"I guess that's the end of the contest," said Nan.

They all went back to the heap of firewood.

Everyone carefully weighed the two bandannas.

"A tie," said Tommy Cheechoo.

"Yes," said Nan, "There'll have to be two surprises."

After they had all had a snack of blueberries, Bert suggested that they make beds.

"How'll we do that?" asked Freddie.

"I'll show you," said Bert briskly.

He pulled out his pocketknife and began to cut some saplings which grew in the shelter of the taller trees. "These are dry enough to use."

Freddie tried to help, but the branches were hard to break off.

"I do that," said the Indian with a smile.

"We'll gather some branches," Nan said quickly. She and the small twins felt around under the trees and collected as many fallen boughs as they could find.

Finally they had three crude beds. "Put your sweater over the branches, Flossie," Nan directed. "We'll use mine for a cover." The two girls snuggled down together.

"It prickles!" Flossie complained as the twigs stuck into her bare legs. But in another minute she was fast asleep.

The boys made their beds nearby and Tommy stretched out a little distance away. All were hungry and cold, but tired enough to sleep soundly through the night.

Bert was awakened the next morning by Nan

shaking his shoulder. "I just heard a plane fly over the island!" she cried. "Do you suppose they are looking for us?"

Bert jumped to his feet, waking Freddie, who sat up and rubbed his eyes. "Where am I?" he asked sleepily.

"We're on the island and Nan heard a plane!" Bert explained hastily. "Maybe we can signal it!"

At this point, the others awakened. As Tommy got to his feet, the children squinted up at the sky. A small plane was circling the island.

"Help! Help!" The twins jumped up and down on the shore, waving their arms, and Tommy shouted weakly. But the aircraft went on, heading toward Moosonee.

"They didn't see us," Nan said sadly.

"Maybe they'll come back," said Flossie hopefully. Her eyes filled with tears. "I wish Mommy was here."

"Now, now," said Nan quickly. "You'll see her soon."

"We'll have to make a signal of some kind," Bert said firmly. "Let's try the fire again."

Hastily the castaways kicked apart the remains of their bonfire and felt among them for dry wood. Soon they had collected a fair-sized pile including twigs and branches from the woods.

"I saw a picture of men who were lost way up

North," Freddie said. "They made a big sign in the snow so the rescuers could find them."

"Good idea!" exclaimed Bert. "We'll fix up an S O S here on the beach that can be seen from the air."

Nan and Flossie quickly brought their sweaters, and handed over the brightly colored bandannas. The boys offered their T-shirts and Tommy gave his blue one. Carefully, the clothing was arranged to form the distress signal, S O S.

"I hope someone will see this before the bad men come with food for Tommy." Flossie looked woeful.

"Or the wind blows it away," said Nan, quickly stepping on a sleeve that fluttered. "We'd better put sticks on the signal to hold it down." She and Flossie worked busily to secure the clothing.

"Can we light our fire now?" Freddie asked.

Bert nodded and took the matches from his pocket. "Get more wood," he ordered. Then he quickly gathered some dry grass for kindling. As Freddie returned carrying another big branch, a small wisp of smoke curled up toward the sky.

"Now we have two signals!" Flossie clapped her hands.

Tommy returned to his bed to rest. The others sat down on the beach near the fire and watched

"I'm sure he saw us!" Nan declared

for another boat or plane. About half an hour later, a seaplane appeared from the direction of Moosonee. It flew up the far bank of the river. The prisoners watched until it was close enough, then jumped to their feet and began shouting.

"Wait!" cried Bert. "All together— one-two-three!" A wild yell went up and Flossie screeched, "Here we are!"

The plane flew on.

"They didn't see us!" Freddie was near tears.

"Look!" Nan was pointing upstream.

The little craft had turned and was flying in lower over the island. Once more the Bobbseys and Tommy shouted and jumped and waved their arms. This time the plane dipped its wings, circled the island, and sped off toward Moosonee.

"I'm sure he saw us!" Nan declared.

"I do hope someone gets here soon," Flossie said.

"How do you think they'll come?" asked Freddie. "Air or water?"

Bert shrugged. "I don't know. Just be patient."

Anxiously the castaways waited.

Time after time Freddie and Flossie went to the very edge of the island and looked up the river toward Moosonee. Then they stared up at the sky.

Finally Bert said, "It'll take 'em a while to get

here. You might as well sit down." But a few moments later he walked over and scanned the sparkling water himself.

As he turned back, he caught the Indian looking uneasily at the sun. Bert knew what Tommy was thinking. It was soon time for the men to return.

Then Flossie spoke up, "Maybe the bad men will come before we're rescued."

Nan looked unhappily at their crackling fire. "Even if we hide, they'll know somebody's here."

As she spoke, Bert gave a shout. "A canoe!"

A craft was speeding down the river toward the island! The prisoners squinted into the sun, trying to make out the figures in the boat.

"I can see a big man in front and two others, but I can't tell who they are," said Nan, shading her eyes.

The same question was in everyone's mind. Was it the three thieves?

CHAPTER XVI

THE MAN ON THE POLAR BEAR

"QUICK!" said Bert. "Into the woods!"

The twins and Tommy Cheechoo ran back among the trees. Anxiously, they watched the approaching boat.

"Hurrah!" Freddie yelled gleefully. "It's Big Moose."

"And Mother and Little Moose," Nan added as the children ran down to the edge of the water and waved wildly. The three in the freight canoe waved back.

"We're rescued!" Flossie shouted for joy as the craft hit the beach. Before anyone could pull it up, Mrs. Bobbsey jumped out and splashed ashore to hug her children.

"Oh boy!" Freddie exclaimed. "Are we ever glad to see you!"

While the twins told their mother what had happened, Little Moose and his father spoke with Tommy in their own language.

"Big Moose," said Bert urgently, "the kidnappers are due back any minute. Now that you're here, maybe we could catch them."

"No," said the big Indian quickly. "Too dangerous! Besides, you and Tommy need a square meal. Little Moose will run you back to Moosonee. I'll wait here. If the men come, I'll hide." He grinned. "When they go to the treehouse, I'll tow away their canoe. Then *they'll* be stranded."

Bert chuckled. "Good idea. We'll inform the provincial police."

Ten minutes later the castaways were speeding toward Moosonee, enjoying the sandwiches and hot cocoa Mrs. Bobbsey had brought. As he ate, Tommy crouched low so the thieves would not see him if they passed that way.

"Did the boy give you our message?" Nan asked her mother.

"Yes," said Mrs. Bobbsey, "but when you didn't come back I began to worry. By evening I was frantic, so I notified the provincial police. It was one of their planes that finally spotted you! Meanwhile," she added, "Big Moose and Little Moose had returned. They wanted to come for you in the plane, but there wouldn't have been room for us all that way."

"I'm glad you came, too, Mommy," said Flossie, snuggling up to her.

On the way Little Moose reported what

Tommy had said on the island: The man with
the scar was the gang leader named Sid Cony.
The bearded man was Ben Gray and the red-
faced fellow was Jack Brenner.

Tommy had been blindfolded on the flight up,
but had heard the men talking. They had spied
on the Bobbseys at the campfire hoping to learn
their plans. Later Jack had seen the young twins
and Little Moose find the gold at Devil Rock.

"So they moved the gold," said Bert.

Little Moose went on to say that the men
found the treehouse by accident. "Some kids I
know built it last summer," he said, "but the
thieves strengthened it."

When they reached Moosonee, the Indian boy
said he would take Tommy Cheechoo home
with him and come back later. While the twins
hurried to their cabin for hot showers, Mrs.
Bobbsey went to the provincial police station
and gave a full report. Then, after a hearty
lunch, the children sat on the front steps.

"I'd like to question that boy who left us on
the island," Bert declared. "Let's find him!"

While Nan and Flossie started toward a
group of children playing at the waterfront, the
boys walked over to the cluster of Indian houses.

Bert stopped a teen-age Indian boy. "Do you
speak English?" he inquired.

"Sure," was the reply.

Bert asked if he knew a boy about twelve who

wore a blue sweater with two big white leaves on the front.

"That was Noah Bluecoat," the boy declared. "His grandmother made him the sweater and knitted the maple leaves in it because they were symbols of Canada."

"Do you know where he is?" Bert asked.

"Probably fishing at Store Creek."

Bert learned that the stream ran along one side of the town and emptied into Moose River. "Mostly we fish just the other side of the railroad tracks," the Indian added. "It's deep there."

The brothers thanked him and hurried up the street toward the train station. They crossed the tracks and walked a short way to a bridge over a rushing stream. Several boys were fishing from flat steppingstones in the center of the creek.

"There he is! I see him!" Freddie shouted.

At the sound a boy in a blue sweater turned around. Two white maple leaves on the front of the cardigan were clearly visible.

"Noah!" Bert called. "I want to talk to you!"

The Indian boy looked frightened. He whirled as if to run, but his feet slipped on the wet rock. The next instant he fell into the swirling water! As Noah's head disappeared the other Indian boys shouted for help. "He can't swim! Neither can we!" one yelled at the Bobbseys.

Quickly Bert stripped off his sweater and shoes, ran down the slope and plunged into the stream.

"Hurry!" cried Freddie as his brother swam to where Noah had bobbed to the surface. Grabbing the boy's sweater, he towed him ashore. Freddie helped the dripping figures onto the bank.

"Thanks," gasped Noah.

"That's okay," said Bert. "But why did you play that mean trick on us?"

Noah looked sheepish. "The fishermen at your cabin gave me fifty cents to leave you on that island. They wished to play a joke on you!"

Bert looked bewildered. "But why would they want to do that?"

"We've never even seen them!" Freddie said.

Noah shrugged. Then he added, "I'm sorry I did it." Before they could answer, he dashed off.

While Bert went to take a hot shower and change into dry clothes, his brother walked to the Lodge. He found his sisters sitting on the steps talking to Little Moose. Freddie told what had just happened.

When Bert joined them, Nan said indignantly, "Let's go see those men. I'd like to ask them about this!"

"They're not in the cabin," said Bert. "I had the same idea."

"Well, I'm going to stay here and watch for

"Hurry, Bert!" Freddie shouted

them to come back," said Nan firmly. The older boys agreed to do the same while the younger twins played nearby. But hours passed and the men did not appear.

It was late afternoon when Flossie suddenly ran over to Nan. "You know what? Freddie and I didn't get our blueberry prizes yet."

"That's right," said Nan. "We'll go to the ice cream stand now."

The five children walked to a small snack booth and joined a crowd of Indian children in bright-colored jackets. The Bobbseys and Little Moose ordered drumsticks, then strolled toward the lodge. The ice cream was cold and hard under a crunchy coating of nuts.

Suddenly Little Moose said, "Here comes my dad!"

The children ran to meet the pilot. "Did the thieves come?" asked Bert eagerly.

"No," Big Moose replied, "but three policemen did. They're staked out on the island now waiting for them."

Nan looked troubled. "I wonder where the kidnappers can be," she said.

"They're around, I'm sure," said Little Moose. "Tommy told me they had to wait here to meet somebody named Harry."

Freddie's eyes grew wide and he nearly choked on his ice cream. He exclaimed, "Harry! The polar bear! The fisherman!"

"What are you talking about?" asked Bert.

Excitedly the little boy told what he had over-heard the fisherman saying on the twins' first night in the cabin.

"Don't you see? Harry—it must be the same man!" said Freddie. His hearers stared in amazement.

"Then the fishermen *are* the three kidnappers!" Bert burst out.

"To think that all the time we were looking for them, they were living in the next room!" exclaimed Nan.

"But what about the polar bear?" asked Freddie, bewildered.

"That's the name of a train," said Little Moose. "The Polar Bear Express. It runs from Cochrane to Moosonee three times a week!"

"They said Harry'd come on Wednesday," Freddie remembered.

"Wednesday!" Bert exclaimed. "That's today! What time does the train get to Moosonee?"

"About four-thirty," Little Moose replied, "but it is never certain."

"We've got to meet that express!" Bert declared. "This is our chance to catch the gang!"

Just then came the sound of a train whistle in the distance.

"There it is now—the Polar Bear!" Little Moose cried.

"I'll go to the police," the pilot said, "and send them to the station. You try to spot the thieves."

The five raced down the road toward the train station. When they reached the long wooden platform, it was crowded with Indians. The men were lined up by the tracks while the women stood in the background. Children were chasing one another up and down the platform.

Seeing the twins' looks of surprise, Little Moose laughed. "Everyone wants to watch the train come in. It is the big thing to do in Moosonee!"

Bert scanned the crowd hastily. Near the station house he spotted the three thieves.

"There they are!" he whispered excitedly.

"They're looking right at us," Nan said. "I'm sure they recognize us!"

The express puffed to a halt and the crowd surged forward. The children held their breath. They saw the man with the scar shake his head slightly as a pale, blond man stepped from the train. The passenger was carrying a knapsack.

The newcomer glanced hastily at the waiting trio, then hurried down the platform.

"That must be Harry!" Nan declared.

"He's getting away!" Bert exclaimed. Just then Big Moose and two policemen ran up. The twins turned to point out the thieves.

They were gone!

CHAPTER XVII

HIDDEN GOLD

THE three thieves had vanished amid the crowd on the train platform.

"Where did they go?" Bert exclaimed as Big Moose and the two policemen looked sharply around.

"There goes Harry!" cried Nan.

The blond man with the knapsack had jumped off the end of the platform and was running alongside the train. Bert and Little Moose darted through the crowd and leaped off the platform with the others close behind.

The blond man broke into a run and sped around the back end of the train. The boys sprinted ahead, but when they rounded the caboose, the man was gone!

"He must be down in the creek," said Bert and dashed to the top of the slope with Little Moose and Nan at his heels. The man was not in sight.

Suddenly Nan pointed to the base of the bridge. Amid a cluster of huge boulders, they could see the top of a canvas knapsack. "He's hiding," she whispered.

Bert and Little Moose sped quietly along the bank until they were above the hidden man. At that moment the fellow broke cover.

"Stop!" yelled Bert, racing down the slope. He leaped and brought the man down in a towering splash of spray as Little Moose gave a warwhoop and came plunging down to help.

Moments later the police arrived with Big Moose and the little twins right behind. The fugitive was hauled to his feet.

"Where are the others?" Nan asked him quickly.

The man set his jaw and said nothing. As the police escorted the man to their headquarters, the twins followed.

"The rest of the gang won't dare go back to the lodge," remarked Nan, " 'cause they know the police are after them."

"They'll try to get away," said Bert.

One of the policemen heard him. "We've alerted all plane owners not to rent to them," he said.

"But suppose they've already hired the plane," said Nan. "We'd better run down to the dock and check."

The children ran to the riverfront. There was

a seaplane with the three men climbing into it.

"Oh, stop them, stop them!" cried Nan, but moments later, the craft soared off the water and flew southward.

The children halted, panting. "We've lost them again," said Nan. Her voice trembled with disappointment.

"Maybe Harry will tell where they went," said Bert.

The children hurried back to the police headquarters. When they reported what had happened, the prisoner smiled. Constable McKensey, the gray-haired officer in charge questioned the man sharply, but Harry would not tell where the rest of the gang was going.

When the thief had been led away, the constable told the Bobbseys that the fellow's name was Harry Kent. Half a dozen bags of gold ore had been found in the knapsack.

"Kent confessed that the gang has been working several mines in Northern Ontario," said Constable McKensey. "They usually split with a miner who obtains the gold ore. But at the Aurora mine they've planted a member of their gang as the 'high-grader.'"

"Did he tell the man's name?" Bert asked.

"No," the policeman replied. "These five men work a place as long as they feel it is safe and profitable. Harry has been picking up the gold from another mine west of Timmins. He told us that much, hoping that we'd go easy on him."

Just then an officer came in and reported that he had searched the room of the three men at the cabin. "We found these," he said, dumping two beards and wigs on the desk.

"No wonder the men were not recognized when they arrived," said Nan. "They *all* had beards!"

"Yes," said the constable, "but they got careless and didn't wear them today." Then the officer thanked the twins and their Indian friends for the help they had given the police.

As they left headquarters, Big Moose said that he would fly the Bobbseys and Tommy Cheechoo to Cedar Camp early next day.

"There's nothing more to do here," Bert agreed.

The twins found Mrs. Bobbsey at the cabin and told her what had happened. Seeing that they were downcast at losing their quarry, she said, "You rescued Tommy and that's the most important thing."

Next morning at dawn the silver craft was winging southward. On the way Big Moose told the Bobbseys that a friend of his had rented the seaplane to the thieves. "He thought they were just fishermen, of course, and had the plane waiting for them as they had ordered. Another customer is supposed to bring it back from Porcupine Lake."

Bert shook his head. "Your friend may never see his plane again."

Big Moose had left his jeep at Trapper Lake. When the seaplane landed there, the Bobbseys and Little Moose waited while Big Moose drove Tommy Cheechoo to Brave Elk's shack. Then he returned and took them to Cedar Camp.

They found Mr. Bobbsey studying some ledgers. He looked up, surprised, as his family trooped in. Lobo ran over to the children, and rubbed against them, whining happily. When the excited greetings were over, the twins told their adventures.

"You found Tommy!" exclaimed Mr. Bobbsey proudly. Then he said Mr. McLain had reported that one of his miners had disappeared. "He's a fellow by the name of Burns—a tall skinny fellow. Jim suspects he's a high-grader."

"Maybe he's gone to meet the rest of the gang," said Big Moose.

"I wish we knew where!" said Nan.

While the pilot drove into Timmins on errands, Little Moose went to Princess Maggie's shack. After unpacking their bags, the twins took a walk with Lobo.

They found themselves following the path to Princess Maggie's. When they reached the clearing, they stopped and gazed at the three holes in the ground.

"From here the gold was moved to Devil Rock," mused Nan. "But where did they take it from there, I wonder?" As the twins walked on, they puzzled over the problem.

Reaching Princess Maggie's shack, they visited a few minutes with the old woman. Little Moose was making a fence for her. The young twins stayed to watch him, but the older ones strolled on with Lobo trotting at their heels.

Suddenly Nan stopped short. "I'll bet the gold is here at Cedar Camp someplace!"

"Why do you think so?" Bert asked.

"Because we saw the men running for the seaplane at Moosonee and they weren't carrying anything with them!"

"It could have been in the plane already," he said.

"Maybe," said Nan. "But there's a chance it wasn't. And if it's around here, I'll bet it's not far from Devil Rock. Gold's heavy and the thieves were in a hurry to rebury it. They couldn't have gone far with it."

Bert looked thoughtful. "There's a made-to-order hiding place close to the rock."

"The old mine!" exclaimed Nan and her brother nodded. "But the men may have picked up the gold by now and be gone," she added.

"If they came yesterday, it was dark by the time they arrived," Bert reminded her. "It's still early. Let's take a look!"

As they quickened their steps, Nan said, "I hope we can find the mine." They trotted steadily through the woods until they sighted Devil Rock. Suddenly they saw a tall, thin figure in a brown shirt and trousers flit past the idol and vanish into the woods.

Bert stopped short and grabbed Lobo's collar. "I've seen him before!" he whispered. "That's the miner who bumped into Cony."

Nan nodded. "I bet he's here to get the gold and meet the others!"

Cautiously the children moved on. Bert remembered in which direction Little Moose had said the mine was. Gradually the trees grew sparser and they found themselves in a large cleared area.

In the center stood a ramshackle, wooden framework. Several shacks stood nearby and an overturned wheelbarrow. No one was in sight.

With Bert's hand on the wolf's collar, the two walked quietly over to the framework. They looked down into a large square hole about five feet deep. One side of it opened into a tunnel which slanted downward into darkness.

"Do you think it's safe to go in?" Nan whispered.

"I don't think those men would take chances," said Bert. "If the gold's there, it's probably close to the opening."

For a moment the twins stood still, listening.

A crow cawed in a tree, but all else was silent.

Bert sat on the edge of the hole and jumped in. Nan followed. They whistled softly and Lobo leaped in easily after them.

With the wolf at their heels, the two stepped cautiously down the slanting tunnel. After a few feet the light grew dim.

Suddenly Bert whispered, "Look!" In a niche in the rock wall was a pile of small leather bags.

"The gold!" exclaimed Nan. Quickly she counted—ten bags!

"We've got to let the police know," Bert said, "and *fast!*"

"But the men may come in the meantime, take the loot and clear out," said Nan. "How can we stop them?"

"Hide the gold," said Bert quickly. "That'll delay 'em."

"But there isn't time to do that and get the police, too," said Nan. "I know!" she added suddenly. "We'll send Lobo to Little Moose for help."

"Good idea," declared Bert. He took a pencil and a scrap of paper from his pocket and wrote a note, telling the Indian boy where they were and asking him to inform the police at once.

Nan rolled the note and tied it to Lobo's collar with her handkerchief. Then she took the wolf's head in her hands. "Go to Little Moose! Understand, Lobo? Run!"

"The gold!" Nan exclaimed

The wolf whined softly. Quickly the children boosted him out of the hole. At once he loped off into the woods.

"Do you think he understood?" asked Nan.

"I hope so," replied her brother fervently. "Where shall we hide this gold?"

"Not the tunnel or the shack. Those'll be the first places the men'll look."

The children glanced around the clearing and at the same time they saw the overturned wheelbarrow.

Bert snapped his fingers. "That's the place! It's such an easy spot, they probably won't even think of looking there."

He climbed out of the hole and, as his sister handed him one small, heavy sack at a time, he hurried over and put it underneath the wheelbarrow.

As they worked, Bert kept a nervous eye on the surrounding woods. The last bag was larger and heavier.

"I can't lift it," said Nan.

"I'll help you," said Bert. He jumped down in the hole.

As the twins bent over the niche in the tunnel, they suddenly heard a gruff voice say, "Well, look who's here!"

They whirled as three men leaped into the hole. "Now we've got 'em!" said the gang leader.

CHAPTER XVIII

LOBO TO THE RESCUE!

BERT and Nan froze with fright as the three men stepped into the tunnel.

Suddenly the bearded man gasped. "The gold! It's gone!"

"What are you talking about, Ben?" said the little man harshly.

"He's right, chief," said Jack. His red face looked worried. "There's only one bag left."

Cony pushed in to see for himself. With a snarl, he turned on the twins. "What did you do with it?"

"Why do you think we know anything about it?" said Bert coolly, though his heart was thumping.

"I guess you were just exploring this old mine," sneered Cony.

Suddenly Nan had an idea. "We saw a tall man in brown clothes passing Devil Rock. Do you think he knows about it?"

"That was Burns," muttered Jack. The men exchanged worried glances.

"He should be here by now," said Cony.

"Do you think he's double-crossed us?" asked Jack.

"He's probably heading for the plane right now!" declared Ben bitterly.

"Right," said the leader. "Ben, you go after him. Jack and I'll look around here just in case these kids hid the stuff."

The bearded man climbed out of the hole and stumbled toward the woods. While Jack grimly blocked the tunnel entrance, Cony took a flashlight from his pocket and went deeper into the old mine.

Finally he came back. "Not there," he said shortly. "I'll try the shacks."

The children waited with their hearts in their mouths. *Would he look under the wheelbarrow?*

Suddenly Cony appeared at the top of the hole. "Burns must have taken it," he said shortly. "I guess he was afraid to come back for that last bag. He knew we'd be here."

"What'll we do about these nosy kids?"

"Take 'em back to the shack," was the reply.

The twins were filled with dismay. How would anyone find them?

Jack heaved the bag of gold out of the hole. Then he roughly helped the twins up. Carrying the sack, he marched them across the clearing behind Cony. As they entered the woods, Bert managed to drop his handkerchief. Both twins stepped heavily, scuffing their moccasins, crushing twigs. They tried to leave a plain trail.

"Pick up your feet!" ordered the big man sharply.

"Okay," muttered Bert, but in a few minutes was walking as heavily as he dared.

When they reached the core shack, Ben was on the porch talking excitedly to another man. The twins' hearts sank. It was the tall fellow in brown!

"Hey, chief," called Ben, "Burns says he doesn't know where the stuff is."

The stranger spoke up in a high, thin voice. "You told me to meet you here. I've been waiting."

Cony gave an angry exclamation. "Get in the shack! Everybody!"

The Bobbseys were herded inside. Ben shoved them onto a cot in the corner.

"Burns, I told you to meet us at the old mine," said the leader angrily. "Why can't you get anything straight?"

The tall man looked frightened. "I'm sorry. I thought you said—"

Cony cut him off with a look. "Are you sure Burns hasn't loaded the loot into the seaplane?" he said to Ben.

"Yes, chief. I checked."

Slowly the four men turned and looked at the children. Nan tried not to let them see how frightened she was.

"All right," said the little man in an ugly voice, "what did you do with the gold?"

Bert glanced quickly about and saw there was no escape. "Under the wheelbarrow," he confessed.

"Ben and Burns, go get it," ordered the little man, "and load it into the plane."

As the two hurried out, the leader sat down at the table and stared at the twins. "You've caused plenty of trouble," he said harshly. "Because of you we had to move the gold from the clearing to Devil Rock and from there to the mine. You made it so hot for us with the police we had to clear out of here fast and take that Indian along!"

"If you ask me, we should have taken the gold, too," said Jack.

"We were safer without it!" snapped his leader, "just three innocent fishermen! The plan was to come back here when the police stopped looking for us." Cony's eyes glittered angrily as he went on. "I radioed Harry to meet us in Moosonee. I thought we'd all wait together there."

Jack spoke up. "But meantime you kids trailed us and made things too hot again."

"I guess one of you broke into our cabin at

Cedar Camp and looked through our suitcases," said Nan.

Jack chuckled. "I did. Made a real mess. We were not only hiding our gold here at Cedar Camp but doing a little prospecting, too. Mr. Cony wanted to find out who the visitors were. We hoped to discourage you from staying."

"Why did you go to the sand claim that day?" Bert asked Cony.

The leader grinned. "I didn't. But I spotted that little blond kid, so I gave a false address. The taxi took me to a clearing where I picked up our copter and came back here to the shack."

Suddenly Jack frowned. "We oughtn't to talk so much."

"What difference does it make?" replied Cony. "We'll be gone before anybody finds these two."

"How did you know we were at Moosonee?" asked Bert.

"The day after you arrived," said Jack, "I went to Moose Factory to pick up some supplies and spotted you at the museum. I followed you to the Indian pilot's house to try to find out if you knew we were here. I wore a mask so you wouldn't know me, but you tore off my lump of pyrite. I was afraid you'd recognize it and guess we were around." Bert told him that the Mountie had the ornament.

"It's a shame the way you treated Mr. Chee-choo," Nan spoke up. "Were you just going to leave him in that treehouse?"

"We'll let someone know about him soon," replied Cony, "but we couldn't go yesterday, because we were making arrangements to fly here, and—" Suddenly he stopped. "Wait a minute! How do you know about the treehouse?"

"Because we found Tommy," said Bert coolly.

The men stared. "How?" demanded the leader.

The twins told about the log ride from one island to another and releasing the captive. "Not only that," said Bert, "your pal Harry was caught by the police. They know all about your activities."

Cony scowled. "I've got a lot to pay you back for," he said coldly.

Suddenly heavy footsteps pounded onto the porch. "All loaded up," called Ben breathlessly and Burns added, "Let's go!"

"What about these twins?" asked Jack roughly.

"Tie 'em up," ordered Cony.

As the men moved toward them, the children quickly stood up and backed toward a corner. Then Jack's big hand shot out and grabbed Bert's arm.

"Let me go!" cried Bert and Nan screamed.

Suddenly a long howl split the air. The men looked startled.

"Lobo!" cried Bert.

At the top of their lungs the twins shouted. "Help! Police! In the shack!"

"Beat it!" yelled Cony, running for the door.

The four men leaped off the shack porch and dashed toward the lake. The children raced outside to see Lobo running into the woods after the gang. Flossie, Freddie and Little Moose came tearing up to the shack.

"Catch them!" cried Nan. "They're getting away with the gold!"

"Wait!" exclaimed Little Moose, grabbing Bert's sleeve. "There's no hurry!"

"Their plane is ready!" exclaimed Bert, pulling loose. "They'll escape!"

"Not without gas in their tanks," said Freddie, grinning.

"What? You mean—"

"We three let the gas out of the fuel drains on the wings," said Little Moose, "I've helped Dad clear water out of the tanks, so I knew how to do it." At an easy trot he led the way to the shore where they saw the seaplane moored.

Lobo was sitting on a pontoon. Suddenly the door burst open and Cony started to get out. The wolf leaped for him, growling. With a yelp the man jumped backward and slammed the door.

Then Jack's big hand shot out

"Good boy, Lobo!" cried Bert. "You hold 'em there!"

"The police should be here soon," said Freddie. "When Lobo came to Princess Maggie's, Big Moose was there. He went in his jeep to get Daddy and the police."

"But they'll go to the old mine," said Nan.

The Indian shook his head. "The police copters will pass over this lake and see the plane. Besides we'll wave to them."

Flossie chuckled. "We found your trail from the mine," she said, and handed Bert his handkerchief.

The next moment two helicopters appeared above Beaver Lake and landed, while the children waved and shouted. Mr. Bobbsey and Big Moose jumped out of one and hurried to congratulate the children.

Meanwhile the thieves and gold were being loaded into the police 'copters. Cony, who was last, jerked around to glare at the children.

"No gas," he exclaimed bitterly. "Another one of your tricks!"

"Inside," said an officer crisply and the angry gang leader obeyed.

Before leaving, Constable Leacock praised the young detectives for catching the thieves.

"Very smart children," said Big Moose with a smile.

Flossie spoke up, "What about the bad men's plane?"

"We'll see that it goes back to Moose Factory," said the Constable. He added that the black helicopter was stolen property and had been restored to its owner.

As the police copters flew off, Mr. Bobbsey turned to the twins and said, "Now that your mysteries are solved, we will have to go home tomorrow."

Everyone looked sad as they walked back through the woods. At Princess Maggie's cabin the Bobbseys said good-by to the old woman.

"You come again," she said, patting Flossie's cheek.

"I'll see you tomorrow," Little Moose promised the twins.

Next morning as the family was putting their bags on the porch, Mike Quinn came striding up the path. "I'll drive you to the airport, Dick," he offered, "and turn in the station wagon for you."

As he spoke, Little Moose ran out of the woods. Behind him were his father and Tommy Cheechoo.

"I bring present," said Tommy, opening his hand and holding it out to Nan.

"Oh, isn't it wonderful!" she exclaimed and held up a small wooden blackbird with four wings.

"He had Brave Elk carve it just for you twins," explained Big Moose. The children thanked Tommy warmly and each shook hands with him.

Flossie flung her arms around the wolf. "Good-by Lobo," she said. "We'll miss you!"

Then Little Moose said sadly, "You will go far away and I must stay on Moose Factory."

"Not this winter!" Nan told him happily. "You're going to live with Mr. and Mrs. McLain and go to high school in Timmins!"

"That's right," Big Moose assured his son quickly.

"Daddy arranged it," said Nan. "The McLains are happy to have you, because you and your father and Tommy Cheechoo helped to catch the gang."

Little Moose was speechless with joy.

"So that was the A-OK secret," said Bert with a grin.

Flossie clapped her hands and cried, "And the funny blackbird started it all!"

ORDER FORM
BOBBSEY TWINS ADVENTURE SERIES

Now that you've met the Bobbsey Twins, we're sure you'll want to "accompany" them on other exciting adventures. So for your convenience, we've enclosed this handy order form.

42 TITLES AT YOUR BOOKSELLER OR COMPLETE AND MAIL THIS HANDY COUPON TO:

GROSSET & DUNLAP, INC.
P.O. Box 941, Madison Square Post Office, New York, N.Y. 10010
Please send me the Bobbsey Twins Adventure Book(s) checked below @ $1.95 each, plus 25¢ *per book* postage and handling. My check or money order for $_____ is enclosed.

SHIP TO:

NAME _____
(please print)

ADDRESS _____

CITY _____ STATE _____ ZIP _____

75-44   Printed in U.S.A.   ☐ 14.

DETACH ALONG DOTTED LINE AND MAIL IN ENVELOPE WITH PAYMENT

This book belongs to

Margaret
Moscato